BABY, COME

Clandestine Affairs 6

Zara Chase

MENAGE EVERLASTING

Siren Publishing, Inc.
www.SirenPublishing.com

A SIREN PUBLISHING BOOK
IMPRINT: Ménage Everlasting

BABY, COME BACK
Copyright © 2014 by Zara Chase

ISBN: 978-1-63258-124-2

First Printing: November 2014

Cover design by Les Byerley
All art and logo copyright © 2014 by Siren Publishing, Inc.

Printed in the U.S.A.

PUBLISHER
Siren Publishing, Inc.
www.SirenPublishing.com

BABY, COME BACK

Clandestine Affairs 6

ZARA CHASE
Copyright © 2014

Chapter One

"It's goddamned suicidal."

"Remember who you're talking to, soldier."

"It's goddamned suicidal...*sir*."

"It sucks," Zeke said, his voice an angry hiss. "Sir."

Colonel Pool glowered at Raoul and Zeke. Raoul and Zeke glowered right back, not giving a damn if their new commanding officer was pissed at their insubordination. *Get used to it, asshole.* As tough, experienced Special Forces Green Berets—the elite of the elite—normal military discipline didn't apply to them. All members of the squad were encouraged to speak their minds about the dangerous missions they undertook in even more dangerous parts of the world. Now some highfaluting command task force comprising US and Israeli top brass had been put together, and they'd had Colonel Pool foisted upon them. Geez!

"Hamas extremists are out to kill the peace negotiations we've worked so hard to set up," Lieutenant Colonel Hassan of the Israeli Defense Force said in a calm tone that only fractionally defused the tension. Hassan enjoyed Raoul's respect. Pool, who was more a politician than a solider and put his own interests before those of the men under his command, did not. "We've been trying to infiltrate their ranks for months, with zero success."

"You don't need to tell us that." Zeke growled.

Raoul and Zeke, with bearded faces and skin tanned by long hours of exposure to the fierce Palestinian sun as they tried to do the infiltrating, looked more Palestinian than American. Right now, in their Israeli headquarters, they had forgone the traditional Palestinian clothing that had become second nature to them in favor of jeans and T-shirts. Even so, Raoul was aware their communal stance projected power, strength, and an ever-present threat of danger, because that was the only way they knew. Pool looked wary of them, which showed he wasn't completely clueless. Raoul could happily detach his head from his shoulders using just his bare hands. The jackass didn't give a fuck about the lives he was putting in danger in his reckless quest for personal glory.

Raoul's wife's life, to be precise.

They knew when they shipped out to Israel that Cantara would be talking to some lethal individuals in an effort to bring all the Palestinian splinter groups to the negotiating table. That was the whole point of being here. But it had slipped her mind to mention that she'd agreed to act as go-between with this particular faction.

"It smells like a trap," Raoul said adamantly. "And my wife ain't gonna be the bait."

"They've asked specifically for her," Pool snapped. "Won't speak to anyone else."

Raoul ground his jaw, furious at Cantara for agreeing to the mission without speaking to him and Zeke first. Knowing why she hadn't. If it was a genuine olive branch on the part of the extremists, it was the opportunity they had almost given up on. Cantara wasn't stupid—far from it—and knew what this could mean for her troubled country. As always, she wasn't thinking about her own welfare. But Raoul and Zeke sure as hell were. Someone had to.

"And you don't find that ever so slightly suspicious?" Raoul asked, not bothering to keep the sarcasm out of his tone.

"Your wife is a well-respected moderate."

"My wife is a *woman,*" Raoul snapped back. "Since when have those misanthropes ever talked politics with a woman?"

"You think they know she's married to you?" Hassan asked.

"I sure as hell hope not. We've kept that knowledge under wraps. She doesn't wear a ring or use my name, but the militants have as many spies dotted about as we do." Raoul shrugged. "I wouldn't bet against them knowing."

"It's too dangerous," Zeke said, his voice a threatening growl that even Raoul found intimidating. "She ain't going."

"She's already agreed," Pool yelled, slapping his fist against his desk for emphasis. "And you are out of line, Orion."

Raoul curled his upper lip derisively. Like yelling and table-slapping was going to intimidate men of their caliber. "And I can get her to change her mind, just like that," he said, walking up to the colonel, crowding his personal space and snapping his fingers beneath his nose. The colonel actually flinched and took a step backward.

"We'll make sure she has good backup," Hassan said. "But we really can't pass up on this chance, no matter the risks. Besides, your wife can handle herself."

"If she goes, then Zeke and I are her rearguard," Raoul said grudgingly, not trusting anyone else with his—*their*—wife's back.

"That's a negative, sergeant," Pool said dismissively. "You're personally involved, which will affect your judgment."

"Damned straight it will." Raoul continued to crowd Pool. "I don't know how else to make you understand this…sir, but unless we're there to watch her back then Cantara doesn't go. End of story."

"You're making a big mistake, Washington, issuing me with threats."

"Sorry to disappoint you, but we don't give a fuck about your ego, Colonel," Zeke said, staring him down. "Our concern is for Cantara, and those are the only terms under which we'll let her go. Take 'em or leave 'em."

Hassan and Pool shared a glance. "Okay," Pool said reluctantly. "You two can be part of her backup team."

"Nope, we *are* her backup team," Raoul said. "We're the best you have, and you know it. The militants will be on the lookout for a tail, but we stand an outside chance of blending in. Any more than two of us, and the whole operation will be blown, to say nothing of Cantara's chances of surviving."

Pool glowered at Raoul and Zeke, clearly more concerned about saving face than saving Cantara. It was Hassan who broke the brittle silence.

"Agreed," he said curtly.

"That's *if* Cantara doesn't have a change of heart," Raoul cautioned.

"Now see here, Washington, don't you go interfering." Pool puffed out his chest, but still looked puny against Raoul and Zeke's rock-hard physiques. "Your wife has agreed to go, and you need to learn to follow orders."

"Unlike Cantara, who is not a part of this man's army, which leave her free to change her mind any time she feels like it," Zeke reminded the colonel, heading for the door without waiting to be dismissed.

"Fuck," Raoul said as they strode away from the commander's office. "You shoulda let me throttle the asshole, Zeke."

"Nah, the army takes a dim view of that sort of thing. I think it's called insubordination. Ask Pool, he's big on all that shit. He's bound to know."

"If they don't want us offing people who deserve to be offed because they're too stupid to live, then they shouldn't have trained us to be killing machines." Raoul threw back his head and groaned. "When I get my hands on Cantara I'm going to…"

"Yeah, buddy, me too." Zeke flashed a brief smile. "Where do you suppose she's hiding?"

"Training ground is my guess." Both men turned in that direction. "It's where she always goes prior to a mission."

"Or when she's done something to get us mad at her."

"Yeah, then too."

Their collective bad mood gave a little as they caught sight of a very familiar figure, taller than average for a woman, dark hair pulled up on top of her head, green eyes sparkling with determination, her body bathed in a thin film of perspiration. She was engaged in hand-to-hand combat with a guy twice her weight and strength—and landed him on his ass. She laughed at his surprised expression and offered him a hand up.

"Gotta hand it to our babe," Zeke said, nodding in admiration. "She knows how to kick ass."

"She'll fucking need to if we can't talk sense into her."

The fight recommenced beneath the eagle eye of the army instructor. This time the guy didn't make the mistake of underestimating Cantara and his superior strength eventually won the day. Laughing, Cantara elevated herself gracefully from the canvas and acknowledged her opponent. She saw the guys watching her and hesitated, just fractionally, before waving and walking over to them. She had a way of moving that hypnotized Raoul, but for once the provocative sway of her slender hips didn't put paid to his bad mood. She knew she was in trouble and he wasn't about to cut her any slack just because his cock got hard whenever he was anywhere near her.

"Hey, guys," she said, a little too casually. "Come to take me to dinner?"

Dinner was not what Raoul had on his mind, but he knew better than to raise that subject of the suicidal mission she had so blithely accepted while they were in public. This was a high-security facility, but still. He slung an arm over Cantara's shoulders and steered her in the direction of their living quarters.

"We need to talk," he said curtly.

Cantara's gaze slid pleadingly in Zeke's direction.

"How come you guys get to be demonstrative in public and I get left out?" he joked, coming to Cantara's rescue. Raoul couldn't blame Zeke for bailing her out, albeit temporarily. When she turned the full artillery of her enormous eyes upon anyone—all vulnerability and smokin' hot woman—the recipient became putty in her hands. Even so, Raoul dropped his arm, as though it had been intended as nothing more than a friendly gesture. It didn't do to flaunt the relationship they were trying hard to keep a lid on.

"Aw, don't feel bad, baby," she cooed. "Once we get inside you shall have my undivided attention."

See, Raoul," Zeke said smugly. "She likes me better than she likes you."

Raoul flipped him off.

"Not better," Cantara replied, flashing a tentative smile Raoul's way, probably conscious of the anger radiating from him since he sure as hell wasn't trying to hide it. "Just differently, is all. You Native Americans can be very creative with your hands..." She giggled. "Well, with all sorts of your body parts. I like that about you."

"Is that right?" Zeke sent her a flirtatious smile. "So what do you have planned for me when we get inside?"

"How about one of my special hum jobs? I know you like those."

Zeke placed both hands over his heart and sighed. "Geez, darlin', just the thought of it is enough to make me come in my pants."

"Oh, don't do that. I'd much rather you came in my mouth."

Raoul and Zeke shared a look over Cantara's head. How the fuck was he supposed to remain mad at her when she talked that way? More to the point, how could he possibly let her go on this mission when there were no rules of engagement within their control? If they lost Cantara, it would be like cutting of their own right arms. She'd cleverly brought the conversation around to sex, knowing it would buy her some time. It would, of course. Raoul was already as hard as

Zeke claimed to be, just thinking about it. They'd have their fun with the woman they would both give their lives for without hesitation, if that's what it took to keep her safe. And then they'd talk some sense into her.

Somehow.

Cantara was a beautiful Palestinian whom Raoul and Zeke had met a year ago when she shipped into their home base of Fort Campbell, Kentucky, under strict security. They had been pissed when their colonel and a spook from the CIA assigned them as her bodyguards. A baby-sitting mission? Seriously? They were way better than that. But their attitude slowly changed when Cantara passed every test of physical durability they threw at her, never once complaining. She earned their respect, and as they got to know her better it became apparent that Cantara was as complex as she was beautiful. As determined as she was damaged.

Intelligent, multi-lingual, and fiercely patriotic, she embraced their lifestyle with enthusiasm, claiming it was the element that had been missing from her existence up until that point. She had always known there was something. Raoul had married her in a Las Vegas wedding chapel six months after they met. It wouldn't have mattered if she had teamed up with Zeke. Both men loved Cantara, knew they had found their soul mate, and needed to prove it by making the ultimate commitment to her.

They had been assigned a two-bedroom, two-bath apartment with its own sitting room in a secure part of the base here in Israel. It had two external doors and Cantara always made sure she went in by a separate one to the guys, keeping up the pretense that they were colleagues and nothing more. You never knew who was watching. They met on the other side of those doors, which opened into the communal sitting room, and where only one bedroom ever got used.

Once they got back to that room, she would become everything she was not in everyday life—subserviently submitting to them both, and doing exactly as she was told. She would expect to be tied up, whipped, punished and then penetrated by them both at once. She had taken to her training like a natural and couldn't seem to get enough of either of them.

Raoul, angry as he was with her impetuous decision to act as referee for warring militants who had their own reasons for not wanting to see peace on the West Bank, knew he would oblige her now by fucking her every which way until she was boneless. He simply wouldn't be able to help himself. She owned him body and soul. She satisfied yearnings that gripped him and Zeke more virulently than a junkie craved his next fix. That was why she absolutely couldn't be allowed to take this assignment.

How to convince her not to, though, that was the question.

"Come on then, beautiful," he said softly. "I hope you realize that you're in for one hell of a spanking."

She sent Raoul a sensual smile and briefly rested her head on his shoulder. "I'd damned well better be," she said. "Sir."

Chapter Two

"You have disappointed me, babe," Raoul said curtly. "Take your clothes off and go crouch in the corner facing the wall while we decide upon your punishment."

"Yes, Master Raoul."

They watched her shiver with anticipation, captivated by the slow sway of her slender hips as she moved to soundless music and did a slow, sexy striptease for them. Her army combat pants and tank-top-covered pretty pink lingerie had both men testing the zippers on their jeans as they growled with appreciation.

"Fuck it!"

Raoul unsnapped his jeans, pulled down the zip and let them hang around his snake hips. He wasn't wearing underwear and an angry erection sprang free, a thick blue vein standing proud down its length. Cantara's gaze briefly dwelt upon it with evident approval before she remembered she was supposed to be playing a submissive role and lowered her eyes again.

Zeke sucked in a sharp breath when she reached for the catch at the back of her bra, unfastened it, but held the cups over her firm breasts, teasing them. Raoul knew what the little witch was doing. Her plan was to drive both of them so wild that they'd forget about talking her out of the mission she'd so recklessly agreed to. Well, she'd gotten their complete attention, no question, but her plan would still backfire. By reminding them of what they had going between the three of them, they were even less likely to let her do stuff that would get her killed.

Still, Raoul thought, sharing a look with Zeke that said *live for the moment*. If anyone had learned the hard way that life was to be snatched by the throat and lived to the full, then it was their wilful Cantara. And right now, Raoul figured she had to be feeling pretty damned empowered as she watched him and Zeke react to her provocation. They were Doms extraordinaire, with the willpower and stamina inherent to that role. One she got into the lifestyle and they promised her monogamy, she bombarded them with questions about her predecessors, insecure because she was convinced she couldn't possibly measure up. Raoul admitted that none of their previous subs had made them lose control in the way she so easily seemed able to, simply by disobeying the rules.

Zeke had unfastened his jeans too, and was gently rubbing his rigid cock as he watched her play them.

"Let it go," Raoul told her.

She licked her plump lips, blew him a kiss and let the bra fall to the floor. Zeke's groans grew louder when she cupped her breasts in her own hands and squashed them together until the beaded nipples almost touched one another. Then she started playing with them, offering them to the guys, but remaining just out of their reach. This was gross insubordination, no question. Cantara knew very well she was not supposed to take matters, quite literally, into her own hands.

"Let 'em go, honey, and lose the panties," Raoul ordered crisply.

Her breasts fell free of her hands, their weight causing them to bounce against her torso as she gracefully stepped out of her panties and threw them at Raoul. He laughed, held them to his nose, and then slid them into his pocket, focusing his gaze on her freshly waxed pussy. Honey trickled down the insides of her thighs. She ran a finger through it, lifted it to her lips and sucked it slowly into her mouth.

"Shit!" Zeke growled.

Cantara flashed another saucy smile, turned her back on them and finally crouched down on all fours, facing the wall, ass poking provocatively in the air. She trembled with expectation as they moved around the room, chatting to one another, deliberately racking up her anticipation by making her wait. They acted as though she wasn't there, stark naked, crouching in the corner, vibrating with a need that only the two of them could satisfy.

When Raoul sensed they had exhausted her patience and she was on the point of doing something rash to speed matters along, they stripped off and approached her. Zeke stood with his feet in the periphery of her vision, while Raoul took up a position directly behind her, rubbing the thongs of a Japanese flogger across her ass. An elongated shudder rocked her body and he knew she would be controlling her breathing and her mind, slow and easy, the way they had taught her, as she waited for the first blow to rain down.

Raoul brought the flogger down hard and sharp, knowing the thongs would spread the tingling across the expanse of her buttocks. He seldom flogged her that hard, so he figured it would give her a good idea just how mad he was with her. She inhaled with a sharp hiss, but otherwise held her position. When Raoul felt satisfied that every nerve ending in her body must be tingling, he grabbed her hair, wound it around his fist, and tugged her head backward while he applied the flogger for a second time. His anger and desperation must have communicated itself because he sensed she was on the verge of orgasm.

"Don't you fucking dare!" Raoul growled.

Zeke fell to his knees in front of her, his throbbing erection grasped in one fist so that it twitched in front of her face.

"Did you mention something about a hum job, beautiful?" Zeke asked.

Raoul released her hair, enabling her to move her head forward, but continued to systematically flog her backside. By canting his head, Raoul was able to see Cantara lick her lips and slide them over the head of Zeke's cock. From his own experience he knew she would be greedily sipping up the drop of pre-cum oozing from it. She then started making a humming noise in a smooth, steady tone—choosing an old Palestinian lullaby with which to torment Zeke— for a few seconds at a time as she moved her mouth up and down his shaft. Zeke groaned as she varied the pitch to create different sensations, just the way they'd taught her. Damn, but she was a responsive student! Raoul felt his own need steadily building, but tamped it down. It would be a sin to rush such a virtuoso performance.

Zeke grabbed one of her tits and pinched the nipple, hard and insistent. Raoul threw aside the flogger and played with her ass— kissing, sucking and biting at the sensitive area he had just whipped. Cantara continued to hum around Zeke's cock. He had to be close but Raoul knew he had superhuman control methods and would spin this out, enjoying the time he spent hovering on the brink. He flexed his hips and thrust himself into the back of her throat. Cantara accommodated that thrust without missing a hum. Raoul's heart swelled with pride. She hadn't even known what a blow job was before she met the two of them. Now she could sing while she drove Zeke wild. Some achievement!

Raoul's fingers, slick with lube, played with her anus, probing and delving. He knew exactly how to ring her chimes and sensed excitement ricocheting through her when he nudged her knees apart. One of his hands reached between them and played with her clit, tormenting the distended flesh. She almost elevated from the floor.

"Keep still, darlin'," he said in a rough, gravelly tone. "And take your punishment."

She mumbled around Zeke's cock when Raoul slid a vibrator into her sopping cunt and switched it on to a moderate speed. Then he penetrated her backside with the tip of his cock. He grabbed her hips and slid a little deeper before withdrawing again, one of his hands pushing the vibrator in and out of her in time with his thrusts from behind.

"Greedy little witch, ain't she?" Raoul mumbled. "She has her mouth, cunt, and backside full of cock, and still seems to want more."

Perspiration transferred from Raoul's body to hers, or was it the other way around, as he leaned over her and nipped at her shoulder blade. She had told them more than once that what they did to her made her feel alive, wanton and desirable. It gave her something to live for again—a circumstance she hadn't anticipated after the annihilation of her family left her dead emotionally.

"You like my cock up your ass, sweet thing?" Raoul asked.

She couldn't speak with her mouthful, but nodded vigorously.

"Steady, sugar," Zeke said, chuckling. "Don't bite the cock that feeds you."

"You're gonna have bruises on your ass from that flogging," Raoul said. "But you only have yourself to blame for that."

As punishments went, it was pretty inept because Cantara *liked* having bruises, if they were inflicted in the name of making out.

"Fuck, Raoul, we need to pick this up, buddy," Zeke said, his voice strained.

"I hear you. Okay, babe, here's the deal. You've behaved badly so you don't get to come."

She made another protest, but with her mouth so full of cock it sounded more like a gurgle. There wasn't any way in the world she could stop herself from coming, and they both knew it. It was just Raoul's way of making his displeasure felt. An excuse to chastise her some more for being disobedient.

"That's it, baby, eat my cock!" Zeke was moving his hips faster, no doubt encouraging Cantara to slide her tongue from his balls to his head and back again. Raoul was pummeling her ass like he'd never fucked it before, taking out his anger on it.

Cantara rocked her hips between the vibrator, Raoul's hand and his cock, bringing all three of them that much closer to the abyss. That did it for Raoul. He simply couldn't hold out and went into spasm at the same time as Zeke, both of them swearing, groaning, and claiming one of her tits to play with. She let go too, swallowing down Zeke's endless flow of semen as Raoul shot his into her backside, his breath hot and heavy against her damp skin. Her body went into spasm and she rode her orgasm like a woman with a point to prove. Like she might never get another opportunity. She released Zeke's cock so she could throw her head back and scream.

"More!" she yelled at Raoul. "Give me more. It's not enough."

"Shit, darlin', you've got it all."

Raoul swept her from the ground into his arms and carried her to their bed like she weighed nothing at all. The three of them lay on a mattress they shared every night, Cantara squashed between their hard bodies. It only took the guys a moment or two to recover their breath, but Cantara was too exhausted to move.

"Shower," Raoul said, tapping her thigh. "Then we need to talk."

Cantara glanced from one of them to the other, took in the rigid set to their features and, sighing, must have known she would be showering alone.

Chapter Three

The guys enjoyed the view of Cantara's ass, striped pink from the flogging she had taken so enthusiastically, as she walked toward the bathroom.

"She's gonna make trouble, ain't she?" Zeke said moodily.

"We'll tie her to the bed if necessary," Raoul replied.

Zeke rolled his eyes. "Yeah right, that'll stop her. She'll enjoy it and demand to be fucked senseless."

"We could withhold our services."

"Speak for yourself. I get horny just looking at her."

Raoul sighed. "Yeah, I hear you, bud."

While Cantara showered, the guys cleaned themselves up and pulled their jeans back on. If they had their discussion in the nude, it could only ever end one way. It was always like that with them when they were anywhere near Cantara. They hadn't yet plumbed the depths of her sensual nature and taught her everything she needed to know about herself and her needs. If she went ahead with this crazy mission, they would most likely never get the chance.

Grim faced, they sat themselves down, side by side, on the settee and waited for her to emerge from the shower. She took her sweet time, probably because she knew what was coming and wanted to delay the moment. Eventually she appeared, hair damp and hanging down her back, almost to her waist, as black and sleek as a raven's wing. She wore a simple sun dress with thin straps, no bra—probably no panties either—and was barefoot.

Cantara looked pale, but composed. Raoul recognized the glint of determination in her eye competing with the satiated expression he was more familiar with. She took the chair they had left for her, directly opposite them, and swung her feet up, tucking them beneath her butt. She winced, presumably because her heels made contact with a fresh bruise, but otherwise showed no reaction. But Raoul could tell she was nervous. The wariness in her expression gave her away, as did the fact that her hands weren't entirely steady.

"Why didn't you speak with us before agreeing?" Raoul asked in a mordent tone.

"You don't consult me when you go on missions."

"That's different, and you know it," Zeke said. "We're soldiers. We have no choice but to follow orders. You *do* get to choose."

"You know why I have to do this." She looked down at her hands and laced her fingers together. "And if I'd mentioned it to you first you would only have tried to talk me out of it."

"Damned straight, we would," Raoul replied, his jaw clenched, square and unmoving, madder than he had been in a long while. "It's dumb-assed, ill-thought out, and plain suicidal."

"Colonel Pool doesn't seem to think so."

Zeke scowled. "Pool wouldn't know his ass from his elbow. He's just out for personal glory and doesn't care about collateral damage."

"Which is all you will be if you do this," Raoul said, team-tagging Zeke's objections.

"It's the best opportunity we've had to talk with the militants for a long time. They're on the back foot right now, their position weakened through recent losses, and they need to negotiate. I can see why Pool and Hassan are so keen to go for it."

"It's not their asses on the line." Raoul growled.

"I can take care of myself. Besides, we knew what I was coming here to do."

"You agreed not to engage with extremists," Zeke reminded her.

"Yes, I know, but…this opportunity might never come around again."

"Oh, for fuck's sake!" Raoul stood up and paced the room. "If that's your attitude then you're dead before you leave this compound."

"I don't plan on dying."

"Why do you think they've asked for you?" Zeke asked.

"Well, I suppose, because I've made no secret of the fact that I want to broker peace in the region. I *am* Palestinian, so I understand the issues." She looked away. "God alone knows, I ought to."

"Then you'll know they don't take women seriously," Raoul said, swinging around to face her again. "Has it occurred to you that they might want to take you out of the equation? You're a thorn in their side, a traitor to the cause in their eyes, an embarrassing female who has forgotten her role in life. Your entire family was wiped out and yet instead of wanting revenge, you work for our side, trying to broker peace."

"I work for both sides."

Zeke flexed a brow. "You think they'll see it that way?"

"It's up to me to make them."

"And what about us? The three of us?" Raoul placed his fists on his hips and fixed her with a searing look. "You don't think what we have is worth preserving, worth fighting for, worth putting first?"

"Of course I do, but—"

"We love you, babe," Zeke said bleakly.

"We never thought that would happen, that we would be able to commit to one woman and be happy, but it has." Raoul raked a hand through his hair. "Shit, if anything happens to you, it would crucify us both."

"Now you're being unfair, trying to blackmail me." Anger flared in her eyes. "How do you think I feel when I see you two going off into dangerous places, never able to tell me where you'll be or what you're doing? I never know when, or even if you'll come back, but I don't try to stop you going."

"We're soldiers," Zeke repeated with exaggerated patience. "It's what we do. We don't have a choice, but you do."

"No." She shook her head. "Actually, I don't."

Only angry breathing on the part of Zeke and Raoul, and anguished sighs from Cantara, broke through the ensuing brittle silence. Raoul knew they shouldn't have lost their tempers, but it was damned hard not to when she insisted upon being so stubborn.

"Are you telling me not to go?" she asked in a small voice.

"No," Raoul replied. "We wouldn't do that. They only time we give you direct orders is in the bedroom, and you don't have to obey them if they make you uncomfortable. What we are doing is telling you we love you, can't imagine life without you, and have this annoying male gene that makes us want to protect you."

"I know that, and I appreciate it, but—"

"We're *asking* you not to go," Zeke said, standing. "And, you're right, we're not above using blackmail. That being the case, you should know that if anything happens to you, our lives will be over, too."

"Oh, Zeke." She stood and threw her arms around his neck. "What can I do or say to make you both understand what you mean to me? You gave me a reason to live, reminded me it was all right to feel things and to risk loving again. You've taught me who I am supposed to be."

"But you would throw it all away on some unrealistic dream?" Raoul asked, his tone now despondent rather than angry. "This part of the world has been at war for centuries. It's rather arrogant of us to assume we can broker peace when so many before us have failed."

"Perhaps it is, but my country means so much to me, especially after what happened to my family. Someone has to try and make the various factions see sense. I didn't tell you before now about this opportunity because I knew how you would be." Her lovely eyes were clouded with pain. "I have doubts, of course I do. I know the risks. What if I'm captured, or killed? What if I never see you two again or, worse, you're captured trying to protect me?" She shook her head. "My heart splinters at the prospect."

"Then why?" Zeke asked, shaking his head in bewilderment.

"Because I think about my family, lost to me forever."

She lifted her chin and fixed them both with a look of steely determination, which is when Raoul knew she wouldn't back down. The solider in him didn't blame her. The man in him wanted to put up all manner of objections. Before he could do so, she spoke again.

"It's time to bring this madness to an end so no other families have to suffer in the way I have. I will do what I have to all the time there's a chance of making a difference, period." She folded her arms defensively beneath her breasts. "It gives me something to live for."

"And we don't?" Raoul shot back at her.

"You know you do," she replied with such pathos in her tone that Raoul found it hard to maintain his anger. "But this is bigger than the three of us." She shook her head. "When my family were annihilated, it left me dead emotionally. I didn't think the part of me that died with my loved ones would ever be brought back to life. And yet, I now have not one but two gorgeous men who fire my passions and help me to put it all in perspective."

"Our pleasure," Zeke said in a muted tone.

"Every time I close my eyes and recall the faces of my parents and husband, their lives wiped out by that stupid bomb, it makes me feel—well, guilty, I suppose."

"Survivor's guilt," Raoul said.

"Right. I would have been in that house at the time, if I hadn't popped out on an errand. My marriage wasn't a happy one but my husband didn't deserve to die any more than my parents did." She sighed, swiping at the tears flooding her eyes. "Then my stupid, misguided brothers, hot headed and out for revenge, joined the local militants—"

"The people you now planned to mediate with?" Zeke reminded her.

"Yes. My brothers both lost their lives on an ill-advised sortie into Israeli territory. The militants who sent them know they miscalculated in sending them. They know I have reason to be mad at them, which is why they owe me, and probably why they asked to speak with me."

Raoul could think of a dozen reasons why that wasn't the case, but knew he would be wasting his breath to voice them. Cantara had grieved for her family, then decided the killing had to stop, which is when she volunteered to help the peacekeeping forces. Someone had to make these war-hungry men understand violence wasn't the answer and there was enough land for everyone to live in peace, regardless of their religious beliefs.

"You say you can take care of yourself," Raoul said, trying another, less emotional, tack. "But you have to realize you won't be able to take so much as a nail file with you for protection. They will search you when they pick you up, then blindfold you so you don't know where they're taking you. Once you get there, you will be at their complete mercy. There is an outside chance they want to negotiate, but no more than that. My guess is that they'll try and turn you, put pressure on you to work for their side. If that fails, they'll treat you as a traitor." He fixed her with a steady gaze. "And you know what they do to female traitors."

Cantara swallowed. "Yes, I do know, and I've thought about it."

"There again they might force you into another marriage with a Palestinian thug loyal to their cause, depriving our side of a valuable negotiator. Just the thought of another man so much as touching you makes me want to hit something." Raoul sent her a searching look. "Or someone. Damn it, Cantara, can't you see, you're being played?"

She left Zeke and walked over to Raoul, reaching out a hand to touch him. Raoul hastily moved out of her range. Both of them were hopelessly addicted to her touch and couldn't think straight the moment her fingers made contact with their flesh.

"Don't go, darlin'," he said bleakly. "Don't leave us."

"I have no intention of leaving you, Raoul, or you either, Zeke." She shared a smile between them, her eyes misty with tears. They didn't return that smile, knowing they hadn't persuaded her and had no choice but to watch her walk off, most likely to her death. "They won't try and hold me. They know it will cause more problems than it will solve if they do."

"You're making the mistake of assuming they're rational thinkers," Zeke said, shaking his head.

"She won't listen to us." Raoul sighed. "Okay, babe, if you absolutely insist upon being involved in this madness, then Zeke and I will have your back."

"No!"

Raoul flexed a brow. "I beg your pardon?"

"No, I don't want you putting yourselves in danger."

"But it's not dangerous, according to you," Zeke pointed out.

"Not for me, so much, but if two Yanks gets caught in the occupied territories—"

"This is not up for debate, Cantara. The only way to stop us is by not going yourself."

"That's not fair."

Raoul glowered at her. "And you're the epitome of reasoned argument?"

"Please, let's not fight." She held up her hands. "We'll all do what we have to do, and there's nothing more to be said. There's a few days left before I need to leave. Let's make the most of them, starting with something to eat. I'm famished. Sex always gives me a ravenous hunger."

Zeke and Raoul locked gazes, shrugged and pulled on their shirts.

"Come on then," Raoul said, holding out a hand to her and sighing. "Let's get you fed and watered."

* * * *

The following days were a blur of activity. Cantara was locked into long briefing sessions with intelligence gurus, telling her precisely what to do and say in every given situation. Raoul grunted when she related some of the stuff they'd told her to expect. She was risking her life and they were treating her like an idiot. Go figure.

The guys kept fit, training until they dropped, determined not to lose Cantara because they didn't measure up physically. In between their respective duties there were frantic bouts of love making, sweet, poignant, and brutal all at the same time, loaded with emotion because they all felt, but did not say, it was important to make every second count.

Cantara became reckless. She wanted to make love outside, on the training course, virtually beneath the noses of the perimeter guards. And so they did. She wanted to lean over the pummel horse in the gym and have her ass whipped, aware that anyone might walk in at any moment. Raoul and Zeke obliged her. She wanted to be fucked in the deep end of the swimming pool. No problem.

They were incapable of denying her anything, and she appeared to know it. No further time was wasted trying to talk her out of the mission. She was as fiercely determined as ever to go. Raoul seriously considered forbidding it. He knew she would listen to a direct order, but she would also never look at him in quite the same way again. He had fallen in love with a reckless, passionate, yet deeply determined woman whose wings he could never bring himself to clip, no matter the consequences.

"This is it," he said when the three of them woke early on the day of the mission. Significantly, they did not make love. "Last chance to change your mind."

Cantara kissed each of them. "I can't," she said quietly, slithering out from between them and heading for the shower. Neither man joined her there.

She was in the bathroom for a long time. When she emerged she was wearing a long, loose dress that completely covered her arms and legs, concealing her figure. Raoul didn't need to see her body. He had committed every curve, every precious dip and hollow, to memory. She wrapped a long scarf—a hattah—around her head, mostly concealing her hair, but still looked as sexy as get-go to Raoul. He and Zeke had used the second bathroom to shower and dress and were both wearing long shirts, belted to indicate they were working class Palestinians. Their pants were loose and they wore long coats over the ensembles. With their tanned, bearded faces they looked just like average Palestinian men, especially when they donned keffiyehes— traditional male Middle Eastern headdresses held in place by circlets of rope known as agals.

No words were exchanged but there were tears in her eyes as she fiercely hugged each of them. They took turns to kiss her, still not speaking. There was nothing more to be said. They left the apartment and Cantara was swallowed up by the intelligence people offering her last-minute instructions. The guys checked their weapons and prepared to leave the compound. She was to catch the public bus to the agreed point where she would be collected. Raoul and Zeke hopped onto a rusty motor bike that looked as though it was about to expire, but its souped-up engine would get them out of just about any trouble they were likely to encounter.

It might well need to.

They left the compound before Cantara and parked the bike a short distance from the rendezvous point a good half hour before she was due to be there. Then they faded into opposite doorways and waited. They saw Cantara step off the bus and walk to the spot where she was supposed to be, right on time. Raoul wondered if he was the only man in the area who could see through her modest clothing to the sumptuous woman beneath it all. Hell, if anything happened to her, he'd tear the Middle East apart looking for justice!

She stood quietly waiting, not showing any outward signs of nerves, but Raoul knew her heart would be pumping, her senses on high alert. He kept a careful watch on the area, but saw nothing to

concern him, as sure as he could be that no one was paying him or
Zeke any attention. Ten minutes after the time when she was
supposed to be collected, a modern-looking SUV pulled up. It had
blacked out windows but when the rear door opened, Raoul thought
he counted three men inside. Cantara climbed into the car and the
driver gunned the engine as he sped away.

Raoul and Zeke double-timed it back to the bike and were two
vehicles behind the one carrying the love of their lives before it
reached the end of the street. They kept well back for fear of being
spotted. Besides, they didn't need to get too close. The car would
head for the checkpoint leading to the occupied territories. Even so, it
made them feel better to keep the car in sight, knowing Cantara was
inside it.

Thanks to perfect papers and advance warning given to the
checkpoint guards, Raoul and Zeke were able to bypass the queue and
were on the tail of the car again very soon after it got through the
formalities. The traffic thinned out as the car continued on its way.
Raoul, driving the bike, was forced to drop a long way back, but that
was no problem. The border guards had placed a tracking device on it
while they searched the vehicle and Zeke, riding pillion, was able to
chart its every move on a mobile device.

Everything was going to plan, but Raoul didn't like it. It was too
easy. Was he inviting trouble by feeling uncomfortable because
nothing had gone wrong? Why wasn't the car taking more precautions
to ensure it wasn't being followed? He sensed Zeke shaking his head
on the pillion seat behind him, obviously thinking the same thing. But
there was nothing they could do about their premonitions, and so kept
right on following the car.

It was driven on for another ten minutes before stopping on the
outskirts of a small town. They pulled off to the side of the road and
he and Zeke took stock of the situation. There were a few people
about, but no one paid them the slightest attention. And no one was
observing them from anywhere nearby, as far as they could tell.

"They've gone into that old building over there."

They were the last words Raoul heard because something hit him hard on the back of the head. Shit, he hadn't heard anyone approaching. How the hell had they stolen a march on him, and had then gotten to Zeke, too?

His legs buckled and he was unconscious before he hit the ground.

Chapter Four

When Raoul regained consciousness, he and Zeke were stripped bare, huddled on a hard bunk in some sort of cellar. It was stifling hot, and there was no ventilation. The air was stale, smelling of sweat, blood and human misery. Raoul's head felt as though it was about to split in two, and his vision blurred each time he tried to move it. What the fuck had they hit him with?

"How the fuck did they get to us without us seeing them?" Zeke whispered, rubbing the back of his own head. His fingers came away sticky with blood.

Raoul held a finger to his lips. There was every possibility of a listening device having been planted in the cell, otherwise they would have been separated. They both spoke fluent Arabic, and had papers to back up their cover story. Their clothing was genuine, and their weapons had nothing to do with the army. But even though their personal possessions were kosher, the bike had a few modifications that would take some explaining.

Raoul knew that wouldn't be Zeke's primary concern any more than it was his. Cantara was the only person who mattered. Shit, they'd failed her at the first hurdle! Raoul's heart lurched when he thought of what she might be going through at that precise moment. She was one of theirs and if they thought she'd sold them out in some way, Raoul didn't want to think about how they would exact revenge.

Focus, he told himself. Regrets wouldn't get them out of this mess. He needed to concentrate on where they were, and how they'd come to be caught so easily. They hadn't been tailed and no one had been paying them any attention when they arrived at this small village. Raoul would stake his life on that. Which meant they had been expected, and their captors must know they were Americans. It explained why they had found it so easy to tail the car Cantara was in, even without the tracking device. They had *wanted* them to follow and Raoul and Zeke had played right into their hands. Fuck it! Very few people knew of their plan, but someone who did had obviously sold them out. There was no way they could have been spotted otherwise. Raoul quietly seethed at his stupidity. If they got out of this alive, he would find the bastard who threw them to the lions and separate his cowardly head from his miserable body.

Two thuggish-looking guys came in not long after they had regained consciousness and one of them jerked his thumb over his shoulder, indicating they should follow him. It was obvious they wouldn't be given any clothes, or the option to politely decline. That was standard interrogation procedure, and Raoul and Zeke wouldn't let it worry them. Strip men of their clothing and you supposedly took their dignity with it. *Nice try, assholes.*

They were led into a larger room, still without windows, but a little cooler and quite well furnished. A guy sat behind a ridiculously ornate desk that was probably supposed to make him look important, playing absently with the papers that had been taken from them.

"Good afternoon," he said politely in English.

Neither Raoul nor Zeke answered him. The man tried again in Arabic and Raoul and Zeke responded.

"It is very courteous of you to learn our language," he said, still in English, "but I happen to know you are Americans, come to spy on us."

When they didn't respond, the men behind them punched each of them in the kidneys. Raoul had been expecting it but it still hurt like fuck. He sucked in a sharp breath but refused to give the guy the satisfaction of falling to his knees. Instead, he glanced over his shoulder at him, committing his face to memory. When the time came, this guy would get his.

It went on for an hour, with Raoul and Zeke refusing to speak, and being thumped each time they failed to. Raoul had long since stopped worrying about letting the blows floor him, enjoying the respite by staying down a little longer each time. The guy doing the thumping appeared proud to have gotten the better of Raoul. Raoul refrained from telling him it wasn't over yet.

"The woman," the head guy said nonchalantly. "She will be remaining here and working for us."

Raoul and Zeke, bloodied and battered, continued to stare straight ahead, neither of them showing the slightest reaction. Somehow. But on the inside, Raoul was gripped by a murderous rage. He chanced a swift sideways glance at Zeke and knew his thoughts must be similarly engaged.

"She is very beautiful and will be suitably married in due course. Why she thought she could interfere with men's work is beyond me, but she has already learned the error of her ways. She will remain at home and produce good, strong Palestinian sons to fight for the cause."

Raoul swallowed, aware that would never happen. The moment they relaxed their guard on Cantara, she would find a way to escape. But the thought of some bastard pawing her until that time came ate away at his gut like a virulent disease.

They were thrown, half-conscious, back into the same cell. They both knew they were being kept together in the hope that they would talk, but really there was nothing they could say that their captors didn't already know. Except they didn't appear to know Raoul and Cantara were legally married. Only Zeke, Pool, Hassan, and Fisher, their colonel back at Fort Campbell, were privy to that knowledge, plus a very few of the support staff. Raoul would stake his life on Fisher being loyal—they had been in too many tight spots together over the years for it to be otherwise. So either Pool or Hassan, or one of the guys under their command, had gotten careless. Raoul's money was on that asshole Pool.

Raoul passed the time by steadfastly not thinking about Cantara. If he allowed sentiment to cloud his mind, they really would be fucked. They were giving swill to drink, a cup of water each, and left alone. Both men drank the disgusting, thin stew. They'd had worse in their time and knew to take whatever sustenance they could get. They would need it because tomorrow things would get worse for them.

And so it proved to be the case. They were routinely beaten, or hosed down with frigid water, just to keep the guards amused. Their bodies were used to extinguish cigarettes. They were deprived of sleep, subjected to ear-splitting levels of noise and even had electrodes attached to the genitals. They endured it by detaching their minds from what was happening to their bodies, because that's what they had been trained to do, all the while wondering if Cantara was still in the building. While that possibility existed, they were not prepared to even think about escape.

The question was answered for them two long days later when they were again dragged before the leader.

"Not quite so sure of yourselves anymore, I see," he said cheerfully, casting an amused glance over their bloodied and bruised bodies. "However, the resolution is in your own hands. As you are well aware, you only need to admit you are American spies, tell us what you came here to find out, and it will all end."

Yeah, Raoul thought, permanently. They would be paraded in front of the cameras and given a public execution on prime time television.

"However, that is not what I wanted to talk to you about." The man casually lifted a tiny cup of thick, black coffee to his lips and inhaled. The rich aroma caused Raoul to salivate, but he kept his expression impassive. "I called you here to inform you of some sad tidings. Unfortunately, the young lady proved to be more stubborn than we anticipated. She refused to join us, or to marry the man we chose for her." He shook his head. "So unreasonable. We have no use for unpatriotic females."

He turned a laptop toward them. Both men called upon their training not to gasp when they saw a gaunt, battered Cantara tied to a chair, defiance in her eyes. A man struck her, she spat at him, and so he struck her again with considerable force. The chair toppled over and Cantara's head hit the ground. Blood pooled beneath it. In the next shot, she was laid on a clean bed, beautiful green eyes wide and staring, but no longer full of sparkle, defiance or any other emotion.

The woman they loved was dead, which changed everything.

* * * *

Back in their cell, the two men huddled together, grieving and seething. They were also getting weaker by the day, thanks to the physical abuse they had endured, and lack of food. They had to get out of here soon, or they never would.

"Tonight," Raoul whispered, knowing there were only ever two guards on at night and that they had become lazy because they thought Raoul and Zeke were too weak to put up any resistance.

Zeke nodded. One of his eyes was swollen shut and his face was as battered as Raoul's, as was the rest of his body. But they were fighting mad, vengeance the only emotion they allowed themselves to feel. They had no weapons other than their bare hands. That was more than enough, even in their weakened condition.

One guard sauntered into the cell with their evening gruel, and spat in it, laughing at how clever he was. It was the same man who so enjoyed beating up on Raoul. Good! Zeke moaned, rolled over and appeared to pass out, blood spilling from the corner of his mouth because he'd taken the precaution of biting his lip, reopening one of the many cuts he'd received over the past few days.

"He's dead!" Raoul screamed in Arabic. He flashed an angry glare at the guard, then felt for a pulse that was actually strong and regular. The guard gaped but didn't move. "Come and check for yourself, if you don't believe me."

Raoul knew they were to be kept alive, either as bargaining tools or for propaganda purposes. Two of America's elite, taken down by poorly armed and trained *freedom fighters* was the stuff to reassure the foot soldiers and send a message to the world. The guards would be blamed if one of them did die, and they knew it. Fear passed through the eyes of the one in the cell with them now.

He leaned over Zeke, who obligingly poked a finger in his eye, directly on target. Before the man could scream, Raoul bashed him on the back of the head and he fell to the floor, his face landing in the lukewarm broth. Raoul knew they had little time to spare, but took a moment to grab him by the hair with one hand and knock his teeth down his throat with the other—payback for all the abuse he'd taken from the slob.

Zeke moved with a speed that defied his weakened condition. He stood behind the door when the other guard rushed in, gun drawn, to see what was going on. Zeke crashed his hand against the man's forearm with such force that he probably broke it. His gun skidded across the floor, and Raoul picked it up.

Silently and swiftly, Raoul and Zeke stripped the two guards, donned their clothing and confiscated their weapons. They gagged them so they couldn't call for help when they came to, took their keys, and locked them in the cell.

"Let's get the fuck out of here," Zeke said, grinding his jaw.

"Soon. But first we have one more score to settle."

Zeke nodded and together they made their way to the room they were taken to when the head honcho wanted to see them. They listened outside and heard voices. A man's, which they recognized as belonging to their tormentor, the one who had ordered Cantara's murder, and the soft laughter of a woman. Raoul nodded, and they burst through the door together.

"When did you forget to knock?" the man demanded in Arabic. He was seated in an armchair with a scantily clad Western woman on his lap. He gasped when he saw who had barged in and pushed the woman aside, reaching for a weapon.

"Don't even think about it, asshole," Zeke said, aiming the guard's gun directly at his head.

"He's mine," Raoul growled.

"No, please. I can pay you. I can help you get away." Tears sprang to the man's eyes as he begged for his life. He no longer seemed quite so tough. The smell of urine implied he'd wet himself. "I could have had the two of you killed, but I did not."

"Your mistake, asshole."

Raoul walked up behind the man, who was quivering with fear, sweat running down his brow. He yanked his head back hard, and saw petrified eyes staring up at him. Cantara. She was all he could think about. The only good thing in his life had been snatched away from him by this sniveling coward. Grief and the burning desire for revenge fuelled Raoul's anger. Using the razor-sharp knife he'd taken from the guard, he sliced the man's throat so deeply and with enough force to almost decapitate him.

Blood spurted, filling the air with its sharp, metallic tang. The woman screamed, but there was no one to hear her. They'd already checked. There were just the two guards at night to keep watch over Raoul and Zeke, and ensure no one disturbed the boss man when he was entertaining his floozy. Raoul had no idea where the rest of the goons he'd seen hanging around slept, but it was presumably close by. He didn't plan on staying around long enough to find out.

"Take me with you," the woman pleaded. "I didn't want to be here. They made me."

Raoul merely shook his head and he and Zeke left the room, locking the door from the outside and pocketing the key.

It was surprisingly easy to slip from the building. They didn't see another person, which was just as well because in their present frame of mind, anyone who crossed their path would not have survived the experience. Outside, the night air was cool, but sweet and fresh after days locked in that stifling cellar.

"What now?" Zeke asked.

Raoul's eyes adjusted to the near dark, and he pointed. "Over there."

"Shit!"

To their utter astonishment, they saw the motorbike they'd ridden parked up in a corner of the compound, the keys still in the ignition.

"Fucking amateurs," Zeke muttered.

"Get the gate. Careful, though. Check for guards first."

Zeke peered through the spyhole, clearly saw nothing, and cautiously opened the gates. Raoul knocked the bike off its kickstand and wheeled it forward. Every bone in his battered body protested but Raoul was running on adrenalin and barely felt the discomfort. Zeke shut the gates again once they were outside, both men astonished that they still hadn't been challenged.

"We must have given a fucking good impression of being at death's door," Zeke said. "Otherwise there would be more guards."

"What worries me is that no one *is* out here on guard." Raoul pointed to a pile of cigarette butts near the gate. "I guess we got lucky and caught them taking a leak, or whatever, but they'll be back any moment. We have to assume we'll be missed and the alarm will be raised." Both men pushed the bike further away from their prison as Raoul spoke. "Shoot if anyone so much as looks at us the wrong way."

"Count on it, bud."

Raoul straddled the bike and started the engine, waiting for Zeke to climb up behind before speeding off, glad to see the tank was still almost full of gas.

Shooting proved to be unnecessary. They made it back to the checkpoint without being challenged. Once there, they got off the bike with hands raised and told the Israeli guards who they were. They were taken into a small room and searched. Then a senior officer strode into the room and smiled.

"Welcome back, gentlemen," he said. "We've been looking for you everywhere."

They were taken back to headquarters, where Pool and Hassan greeted them. Pool looked justifiably anxious. They showered, had the worst of their cuts attended to, moodily subjected themselves to physicals and then ate something. After that, in spite of the fact that it was three in the morning and they hadn't slept properly for the week they had been held, they confronted Pool and Hassan again.

"Cantara is dead," Raoul told them in a flat tone.

"I am so very—"

"Don't you fucking dare offer me condolences!" he yelled at Pool. "I told you what would happen…I warned you."

Hassan sighed. "How did they get on to you, and how did you escape?"

Raoul was grateful for his professionalism. Facts he could handle, and they spent an hour retelling everything that had happened to them.

"So," Raoul said at the end of the debrief. "The question remains, which of your trusted inner circle sold us out?"

"You must have gotten careless, let someone see you," Pool said. "I told you it was a bad idea for you to go."

Zeke had to hold Raoul back. Otherwise he would probably have spent the rest of his life in another prison cell for killing the bastard.

"Don't you fucking dare question our professionalism, *colonel.*" He growled.

"Get some sleep," Hassan said, hastily stepping between a snarling Raoul and Pool, whose entire face had drained of color. "I'll start asking questions and will know more by the time you wake up."

"Let's hope so," Raoul replied, "because, I gotta tell you, if you don't find the mole, we sure as hell will, and I wouldn't want to be in their shoes when we do."

Raoul and Zeke slept for a few hours in quarters other than those they had shared with Cantara. They would never go back to those. Even so, Raoul had his sleep haunted by images of the woman they loved, and was sure Zeke did, too.

They looked a little better when they woke but felt worse after six hours in the sack than they had before they hit it. Realization had struck home. Cantara was gone. They would never see her beautiful face again, and Raoul would never forgive himself for allowing her to go on the mission. He felt tears prick the back of his eyes and made no effort to hold them back. He had known, known, it wouldn't work. He should have tried harder to convince her of that. Damn it, he was an idiot!

They took breakfast then reported to Hassan.

"I have found the man who betrayed you," he said in a hard, crisp tone. "My adjacent, Levi."

Raoul nodded. "I thought it had to be him. It had to be someone at this end of the operation and he seemed like the most obvious candidate."

"Why did he do it?" Zeke asked. "No, let me guess. He got caught in a honey trap."

"We think so."

"Christ, how could he be so fucking stupid?" Raoul asked. "People in his position are prime targets. Surely he knew that?"

"Evidently not." Hassan sighed. "He isn't talking, yet, but we've searched his stuff and it's looking like there was a woman involved. All sorts of intimate e-mails to a female who isn't his wife. We're checking it out." He shook his head. "The man's been with me for years. I thought I could trust him absolutely. It just goes to show." He stood up. "Gentlemen, I am so very sorry but, if it helps, Israeli justice is swift and brutal."

"Give me five minutes with him," Raoul said. "I'll save you the trouble."

"Sorry, but you know I cannot."

"Just five minutes, come on, you owe me that much after we put our necks on the line for you. Five minutes is all I ask. Come on, come on, I…"

Chapter Five

Raoul woke with a start, pulled from his recurring nightmare by the sound of his own voice crying out for five minutes with the man who'd ruined his life. With the sheet twisted around his body, he was covered in perspiration, and racked by the devastating pain of loss. He sat up and ran a hand through his hair. Shit, would it never go away? It had been three years now, and he thought he had gotten over the worst of it—if a person ever really did get over that sort of loss. The guilt, the what-ifs, the regrets.

The sex…dreaming of it felt as though it had happened yesterday. He felt her emotions, her reactions, lived her thoughts—at least in his dream. Only in his dreams. His dreams were the only place he could still be close to his beautiful, wilful wife, and he never wanted to part with them, even if they left him feeling the raw grief all over again when he woke up. He gazed at the opposite wall to his bed, where he had hung an enlarged black and white photograph of Cantara, her head tilted playfully, her sloping eyes sparkling with mischief. It was the first, the only, thing he wanted to see when he opened his eyes each morning.

"Come back, baby," he muttered, his eyes moist. "I can't hack it without you. Neither of us can."

Zeke was hurting too, but unlike Raoul he did his grieving mostly in silence. His Native American belief that Cantara's soul had passed to the spirit world and that she would be reincarnated helped him to get through. Raoul wished he had a faith network to lean on, but he'd seen too much crap go down in this world to believe the next one would be any better—if there even was a next one.

"Fuck it, darlin', why didn't you listen to us?" he asked her picture. "Why did you insist upon leaving us?"

Now that he was awake, he remembered why the nightmare been so vivid this time. It was exactly three years ago today since she had been taken from them. He and Zeke had celebrated the anniversary eve by getting wasted and not talking about it. Raoul still almost tore his buddy's head off whenever he mentioned her name. In Raoul's case, talking most definitely did not ease the pain. Instead, it just reinforced his devastating loss.

With a jackhammer beating away inside his skull, he got out of bed, opened a drawer, and took out the only thing he kept in it. The pink panties that Cantara had recklessly thrown at him on the day she did her striptease for him and Zeke. They were his talisman, his lucky charm, his remaining connection to the love of his life. Zeke tried all the time to get Raoul to move on with his life. To find someone new and start again, but Raoul couldn't do it. There wasn't another woman on the planet who could replace Cantara, or erase his guilt for letting her down. And for all his talk, Raoul knew Zeke felt the same way.

Besides, there was unfinished business they needed to attend to before they gave any thought to their long term future.

Levi, the man who had caused Cantara's death by leaking word of her marriage to Raoul to the wrong people, had escaped from Israeli military detention and was still on the run. Raoul shook his head, mindless of the headache pounding at his temple. So much for Israeli swift and brutal punishment. They couldn't even keep one man locked up. Someone had to have helped the guy, Raoul reasoned. Presumably the same people who persuaded him to turn traitor. He and Zeke needed to stop feeling sorry for themselves and assuage their guilt by finding the answers that continued to elude them. No more hanging out in Wyoming, waiting for something to happen. It was time to be proactive. They would exact justice for Cantara, cut down in her prime, when all she had wanted to do was make a difference to a troubled part of the world that she loved so much. It was the very least they could do to keep her memory alive.

Levi had left his wife and family and hadn't been heard from since he went on the run. Allegedly. Raoul wasn't sure he believed that, so it might be time to pay Mrs. Levi a personal visit and put some pressure on. He had people looking everywhere—places where the average citizen would never gain admittance—convinced Levi would surface eventually. But so far he hadn't. It took money and influence to disappear completely when so many people wanted you found.

"We'll get the bastard, babe," he said, rubbing the panties against his cheek, convinced her perfume still lingered on them.

He replaced them carefully and wandered into his bathroom to splash water on his face before diving into the shower and turning the jets to freezing—a surefire hangover cure. He forced himself to endure the cold water cascading down on the top of his head for two minutes, distracting himself by recalling what had happened after Levi's escape and Pool's embarrassing efforts to save face. The man was a walking disaster area, Raoul thought as he gratefully shut off the faucet, stepped from the shower stall, and vigorously rubbed his limbs to install some warmth into them.

When it became apparent that nothing was being done to track down the people who had taken Cantara for fear of derailing the peace talks, such as they were, Raoul and Zeke became totally disillusioned. They decided they'd had enough of taking orders from incompetent men like Pool and that it was time to dish them out instead. They wanted out, and forced Pool's hand to make it happen, even though they both officially had time to serve.

They left the army and set up the Clandestine Affairs Investigation Agency, which they ran from their high-tech ranch buried in the Wyoming countryside. It was manned by tough ex-forces guys for whom kicking butt was a way of life. Few people knew of the agency's existence, and Raoul and Zeke were very selective about which assignments they took on.

Raoul didn't need a shrink to tell him why he had decided to become an investigator. His operatives worked under the radar, obeying no one's dictates other than those of their own consciences, delivering their own form of justice that didn't allow the guilty to escape. The irony was that a lot of their assignments now came from the military hierarchy, who couldn't be seen to get involved in sorting out their own screw-ups. Raoul took pleasure in charging top dollar to clean up after them.

He had managed to right no end of wrongs—except the one that mattered the most. Despite all the money and expertise he had thrown into the search, he still hadn't found Levi.

But, he decided, his jaw jutting with determination—that was about to change.

Raoul pulled on his normal uniform of jeans and T-shirt and wandered into the kitchen, unsurprised to find that Zeke already had the coffee going. They had spent hours planning their retirement to Wyoming, Zeke's home state, where he was brought up with the Arapahos. Cantara loved horses, so Zeke and Raoul bred horses, imagining Cantara there with them, black hair streaming out behind her as she galloped hell for leather across the endless plains of their ranch. She would have loved every minute of it.

She would never get to see it.

"Tough night, bud?" Zeke asked, pouring Raoul a cup of strong, black java.

"Yeah. You?"

Zeke nodded. "It don't get any easier."

"Tell me about it." Raoul prowled around the spacious room, moody and restless, feeling like something significant was about to happen. "Where the fuck is Levi?" he asked.

Zeke didn't answer, probably because it was a rhetorical question Raoul had asked dozens of times before that frustrated the hell out of them both. The sound of their private line ringing cut through the ensuing silence. Few people had that number, and when it rang it usually spelt trouble. Still, today of all days, trouble was what he was in the market for. Raoul, spoiling for a fight, pushed the button for the speaker phone.

"Yeah," he said.

"Washington?"

Raoul exchanged a glance with Zeke, wondering if he was going insane, or if he was still dreaming. He had never expected to hear that voice again, mainly because he thought the man who owned it was too cowardly to speak to him. Not that Raoul had anything to say to the bastard, but still…

"What the fuck?"

"I take it it's you. This is Colonel Pool."

"I know who it is," Raoul replied, grinding his teeth. "I just wondered at your gall, calling at all, but especially today."

Zeke placed a restraining hand on Raoul's arm. Just as well, otherwise Raoul might have damaged a very expensive high-tech phone by throwing it across the room. They both knew Pool had been reassigned following the debacle on the West Bank, and he had been riding a desk at the Pentagon ever since. What was less clear was why he chose to call them.

"I have a good reason for getting in touch."

"So I should fucking hope."

"Er, the thing is, I thought you should know, a house on the West Bank was raided by our forces a couple of days ago following a tipoff. We found a prisoner there."

"Levi?" Raoul asked, hope flaring.

"Negative. The prisoner was a woman. She doesn't remember anything about how she got there, or anything much at all, but…well—" Pool noisily cleared his throat. Raoul flashed a look at Zeke, who appeared equally bewildered. "I don't want to get your hopes up, but our people on the ground think it might be your wife."

Raoul, who had withstood a week's torture at the hands of the freedom fighters and barely shown any reaction, felt his legs give way beneath him. He fell into a chair and shared an astounded glance with Zeke. It couldn't possibly be true. He'd seen her dead body with his own eyes, albeit on a computer, but he knew enough about death not to be fooled by a ruse. Didn't he?

"Is this some sort of sick joke?" He growled.

"I don't expect you to believe this, but I feel real bad about what happened to you guys, and to your wife, Washington. I wouldn't have made this call unless we had good reason to hope."

"You met her often enough," Raoul said. "Surely you would know if it's her."

"I think it is, but she's been through a rough time and, if it is her, her appearance has changed a lot."

"Fuck!" Raoul muttered.

"You say she doesn't remember anything," Zeke said.

"Not even her name. But she keeps mumbling something that sounds like your name, Washington."

"She says Raoul?"

"Far as we can make out. And Ze." The guys shared another protracted look. Raoul didn't want to get his hopes up, because he didn't think he could stand the pain of disappointment. Even so, a gasp caught in his throat, while his heart thumped faster than his pulse. Cantara's pet name for Zeke was Ze. "She's sedated, a bit delirious, but our people are sure she's muttered the word *Wyoming* once or twice."

Even Zeke's swarthy complexion had paled. "Do you have a picture?" he asked Pool.

"Yeah, but like I say, she—"

"Send it to us right now!" Raoul yelled.

Raoul and Zeke stood by their computer, trembling with a combination of anxiety and anticipation as they waited for the picture to come through. Zeke muttered a few words in the Arapahoan language. Raoul merely muttered as he twisted the fingers of both hands together so tightly they were in danger of dislocating.

"If this is a wind-up, I'll go to the Pentagon and this time you would be able to stop me from breaking his miserable fucking neck." He growled.

"You'll need to stand in line, bud."

"Shit, what's taking so long?" Raoul glared at his computer, willing the e-mail to come in. "This waiting is fucking killing me."

"Do you really think it could be her?" Zeke asked.

"I honestly don't know." Raoul shook his head, wondering now if his especially vivid dream was attributable to more than just the dateline. If his sixth sense had picked up on something, why the fuck had it waited so long? He hadn't doubted for a moment that Cantara was dead. "That video we saw looked real to me, but…hell, it never even occurred to me to think she could still be alive. The Israelis raided the place where we were held and it was deserted, no sign of her, and nothing to lend a clue as who it was who'd been there."

"That's what they told us." Zeke growled. "Perhaps we were too trusting."

"Fuck, I never would have left the region if I'd had the slightest inkling she might still be alive."

"Me neither."

Raoul ploughed a hand through his hair, calling himself all sorts of an idiot. "How could we not have thought about it, Zeke? Asked more questions? Probed more deeply? We're supposed to be highly-trained professionals. It's what professionals do. They question everything."

"I don't know why we didn't do that, buddy. We were pretty psyched up with grief, I guess, and actually believed what we were told. We ought to have known better, but we also knew they wouldn't hesitate to kill her if they even suspected something was off about her." He shrugged. "If they somehow found out the two of you were married, that would be enough—"

"Shit!"

"Right, we believed our own hype. We made a rookie error. If it is her."

"You think the brass knew and didn't tell us?" Raoul asked, gripped by a murderous rage.

"Dunno. It would account for why they let us get out before our time, I guess."

"They didn't want us around to ask awkward questions."

"Yeah, most likely." Zeke looked as bewildered as Raoul felt. "Still, first things first. Let's not get our hopes up, but we do need to know if it's her."

"Yeah, we do." Raoul tapped his foot, praying to a God he didn't believe in to give him a second chance. His vivid dream was still with him—her beautiful sloping eyes alight with passion, a sultry smile playing about her lips as he threatened to whip her ass...damn it, was that why he hadn't been able to let go? Had he known, on some visceral level that she was still alive? *If* she was. "Come on, come on, what's keeping him from sending that damned picture?"

An e-mail popped up in Raoul's inbox just as the words slipped past his lips. Both men paused when they saw it was the one they were waiting for. Raoul's hand was shaking as he clicked the button to open it. He exchanged a glance with Zeke as his finger hovered over the attachment.

"You ready for this?" Raoul asked.

"I've been ready for three years. I guess I just didn't realize it."

"Me neither."

Raoul drew in a ragged breath and opened the attachment. As he did so he looked at Zeke, rather than the image that sprang to the screen. Zeke was looking right back at him, obviously too scared to have his hopes dashed, too.

"Together," Raoul said softly.

Zeke nodded, took his own turn to inflate his lungs and together they looked down at the screen, from which the face of a gaunt female stared back at him. A defeated female who was a total stranger to Raoul. The disappointment was so intense that he was unsure if he could withstand it.

To distract himself, he took another look, trying to find some empathy for all this poor woman had obviously suffered. She had dull green eyes that sloped, high cheekbones that jutted, a cute turned-up nose. Raoul's breathing hitched. He had kissed that nose more times than he could recall. She looked half-dead, haunted by a thousand demons, suffering and deprivation evidenced in her expression. But now that Raoul was looking properly, he couldn't believe he hadn't known her immediately.

The love of their life was alive!

"It's her," they said together. "No question."

Chapter Six

"It's her," Raoul repeated into the still open phone line. His voice sounded as raw as his emotional state. "Where is she now?"

"In a medical facility in Israel."

"We're going out there."

"No need, she's fit enough to come home. I needed to be sure she is who I thought she was before I got her back stateside. Now that I am sure, I'll make arrangements for her to be flown into Andrews."

"We want to be there."

"Understood. I'll call you right back."

Raoul and Zeke slumped at the kitchen table. Both of them had moist eyes. Raoul felt overwhelmed by joy, panic, but most of all, guilt.

"We let her down, bud." Raoul shook his head. "We made a basic stupid fucking mistake. We believed what we were shown and left her to suffer in some hellhole all this time." He crashed his fist against the granite surface. "Fuck! I hate to say it but that asshole Pool was probably right to say we were too close to her to be objective. If it had been anyone else, would we have believed that video?"

"Yep, most likely." Zeke nodded emphatically. "Even if we didn't, we would have known there was fuck all we could do to pull her out."

Raoul scowled at his buddy. "You might not have been able to, but—"

"Let's just enjoy knowing she's alive for now," Zeke replied in a placating tone. "There'll be plenty of time for recriminations later."

"Yeah, she's alive, but has lost her memory."

"She hasn't forgotten our names," Zeke pointed out. "That's just typical of our little gal, if you ask me."

Raoul managed a grim smile. "I can't bear to think about what she's been through. It makes me feel like such a fucking failure." He raked a hand through his hair. "She clung on to our names, but shut everything else out, and yet we had no idea. Not a fucking clue. We should have known she was alive. She's our soul mate." He glanced at a framed picture of the three of them on their wedding day that he kept beside his computer. The guys were suited and booted, each with an arm around Cantara's slim waist. The bride looked radiant, smiling widely as she clutched a tacky balloon she had refused to part with all day proclaiming her to be *just married.* "Damn it, we should have sensed it."

"Perhaps we did, which is why we've never been able to move on."

"Yeah, could be, but we never would have hung around here if we'd known she was still in Palestine."

"Damn straight we wouldn't have, but we can't change the past. All we can do now is concentrate on getting Cantara home and making sure she has the very best of everything."

"We need to find a neurologist for her. The very best there is."

"That we can do." Zeke stood up, pulled Raoul to his feet, and engulfed him in a man-hug. "She's alive, bud. We'll get her back and we'll spend every dime it takes to get her well. Focus on that."

Raoul slapped Zeke's shoulder. "Count on it."

Raoul picked up the phone and called the local airfield. "Get the plane fuelled up, Pete," he told the guy who answered. "We'll be taking off for a while, probably this afternoon."

"They'll never let us land the Lear at Andrews," Zeke pointed out when Raoul hung up.

"No, I'm fixing to fly us into Dulles."

"Good idea, but bear in mind they might not even let us move Cantara out. They'll wanna hold on to her."

"They're welcome to try." Raoul growled. "I ain't leaving her. Not again. If she's well enough to fly all the way from Israel, she sure as hell is well enough to come back here, where we can look after her right."

"I'll start looking for a neurologist," Zeke said, firing up his own computer.

"When we know what specialist needs she has we can arrange for nurses, if necessary." Raoul picked up the phone to call Dulles, making arrangements to fly their jet into the private area of the busy airport. They were given clearance to land at six that evening.

"Okay, I've found the guy we need. The neurologist. I'm gonna call his office now."

"Not much point until we know when we can get Cantara to see him," Raoul replied. "Just see how available he is. See if we can get him on standby. Don't care what it costs."

Zeke used his charm on the doctor's receptionist and actually managed to get to talk to the man himself.

"He sounds intrigued by Cantara's case," Zeke said when he hung up. "He promises to be available the moment we get her here."

"Good to know."

"Dulles is eighteen hundred miles," Zeke said, doing the calculations in his head. "Even easing back on the throttles we can do it in four hours, easy."

"Right. We'll grab a hotel tonight and be at the base in good time tomorrow."

"Sounds like a plan." Zeke sat down, stretched his long legs out and planted his feet on Raoul's desk.

"How do you manage to stay to calm?" Raoul demanded to know.

"There are colors and feelings and emotional terrain that we occupy that is ours and ours alone," Zeke replied cryptically.

Raoul shot him a look. There was no getting through to Zeke when he went all Zen on him. He paced the length of the room repeatedly, his mind whirling, his emotions on overload. Cantara was alive! She was alive. He repeatedly looked at her gaunt image on his computer screen, becoming more agitated by the minute. Zeke, on the other hand, appeared to fall asleep, but Raoul knew he would be feeling every bit as anxious. He was just better at covering it.

Time seemed to stand still as they waited for Pool to call them back with details.

"Come on, what the fuck's the holdup?" Raoul demanded to know.

"Red tape, a million forms, logistics." Zeke opened one eye and shrugged. "You know how it is."

"Don't I just."

Two hours later, the phone finally rang again.

"She'll be arriving at Andrews fourteen hundred hours tomorrow."

"We'll be there. Get us clearance."

"Do you need transport from the airport?"

"No, we'll make our own way."

"Er, Washington, don't expect too much."

Raoul's body stiffened. "You know something more about her prognosis?"

"No, you know as much as I do." *That'll be a first.* "I'm just saying, that people who have been held captive for a long time, especially if they've experienced a head injury…well, they're not always the same afterwards."

"What do you know about where she was held and by whom?"

"We'll talk in person."

"You'll be there tomorrow? No more sandbagging, Pool. We need some answers."

"I'll be there. Call me if you need anything before then and I'll make it happen."

"Better late than fucking never," Raoul muttered as he input Pool's private number into his cell and cut the connection. "Why do I still not trust that jerk?"

"Because he's still the same old bundle of joy."

"He knows a damned sight more than he's letting on. He always has, and we let him cut us out." Raoul flexed his rigid jaw. "Those days are over."

"I hear you, pal. I hear you." Zeke elevated himself effortlessly from his prone position and landed soundlessly on his feet. "Come on, bud. We don't know how long we'll be away for. We need to make arrangements."

They cut across the back of their ranch, to the converted barn occupied by Mark and Karl, two more ex Green Berets. They ran the day-to-day side of the Clandestine Agency's business from living quarters stuffed to the brim with state of the art equipment—some of it actually legal. They could trace just about anything that moved, and hack into almost any system known to man. Oh, and in their spare time they acted as ranch hands.

"What's up, guys?" Karl asked as Raoul and Zeke strolled into their domain.

"We're gonna be gone a few days," Raoul replied.

"Okay, there's nothing we can't handle going on right now."

"Going somewhere nice?" Mark asked.

"Kinda."

Both guys looked stunned when Raoul told them. "She's alive? Shit, man, that's great!" Karl said, leaping to his feet and shaking both their hands. The guys were also into the ménage scene and knew what Cantara had meant to Raoul and Zeke. "Get out of here and leave the grunt work to us."

"We're on our way," Zeke replied, heading for the door.

"Bring her back safe," Mark said. "We're here for you guys."

"We know," Raoul told him. "And we appreciate it."

An hour later Raoul was in the pilot's seat of their private Lear jet, doing the final checks prior to take off. Zeke was strapped into the co-pilot's seat. Raoul taxied away from the hanger and received take-off clearance.

"Okay, bud," Raoul said into the microphone attached to his headset. "Let's go bring our baby home."

* * * *

They cleared security at Andrews by noon the following day. Pool was there to meet them. So too was Hassan and Agent Parker, the CIA spook who had sanctioned Cantara for her role as intermediary in the peace process almost four long years ago. Part of Raoul wanted to rip him apart for making that decision, even though the rational side of his brain told him he never would have met her were it not for Parker. Would it be better not to have known her, to have loved her, but have her alive somewhere in the world?

The men shook hands all around and followed Pool into a conference room.

"What more can you tell us?" Raoul asked the moment they were all seated. He ignored the coffee that was placed in front of him, unable to eat or drink a damned thing until he knew more.

Hassan's expression was terse. "She was being held in the cellar of a private house."

Raoul and Zeke both nodded. "Yeah, Pool told us that much."

"Er, what he didn't tell you was that the house belonged to her brother-in-law."

Raoul and Zeke exchanged a loaded glance. "She mentioned that her husband had a younger brother," Raoul said slowly. "He worked as her husband's research assistant at the university. She described him as small, quiet, and insignificant. Far as I know, neither he nor her husband had anything to do with extremist groups."

"The husband didn't, but his younger brother was a different matter," Hassan replied. "Seems he was pretty hooked on your wife, Washington."

"The hell he was." Raoul growled.

"You mean he arranged for her to be taken," Zeke said, "so he could..."

"We do know he was closely associated with the extremist group that Cantara went off to have talks with. In fact, our information is he's the one that got her hot-headed brothers to join that group when her parents and his brother were killed by that bomb."

"And got them killed in the name of the glorious cause as well," Zeke snarled.

"Right." Hassan rubbed his chin. "We underestimated this guy, gentlemen. We knew about him, of course, but he played the role of the subservient little brother so convincingly that we never realized what a devious little bastard he actually was."

"Was?" Raoul queried.

"He blew his own brains out when we raided his house." Hassan shrugged. "Just as well he did because we think the first bullet was intended for your wife, Washington, only we got to him before he could use it. He intended to take them both out in his twisted version of a lovers' tryst."

"Christ, what a fucking mess!" Raoul dropped his head into his splayed hands and shook it from side to side.

"That about sums it up," Hassan said. "This guy, Salim, heard Cantara wanted to parlay with his buddies, and took matters into his own hands. He must have found out from Levi that you were her backup and that she was married to you, Washington. Now, we have to assume that Salim wanted to show Cantara the error of her ways and persuade her to marry him instead, so they could breed lots of little Palestinians loyal to the cause. We know this because we found a locked room in his house plastered with pictures of her, taken when she was married, but obviously without her knowledge. He'd built a shrine to her, so we're guessing he wanted it all to be pure and perfect between them."

Zeke snorted. "Yeah, like Cantara would play along with that."

"Which is probably why he turned to violence, which would explain the skull fracture," Agent Parker said. "From what we've subsequently learned, he was a bit of a sociopath, meek and mild on the surface, as cold and hard as ice beneath it all. Except when it came to Cantara. Everyone has an Achilles heel, and she was his. He'd probably decided she wanted to be with him as much as he wanted her, but when she rejected him, he couldn't handle it and the cruel side of his nature surfaced."

"Are you absolutely sure he's dead?" Raoul asked in a murderous tone.

"Yeah, he's six foot under," Parker replied.

"Pity," Zeke muttered, a chilling cast to his expression.

"So why didn't they take us both out when they had the chance?" Raoul asked. "That would have resolved the problem of Cantara already having a husband. They were expecting us and had the drop on us. They could have done it easy with a long-range rifle."

"We think Salim had to do some horse trading with his buddies. He got to whisk Cantara away but they got to keep you two. Two prize Green Berets to use for propaganda purposes. That must have been a pretty compelling reason to give Cantara over to Salim. Unfortunately, you selfishly spoiled their party before they could capitalize on their gain."

"It's just fucking crazy enough to make sense," Raoul said to Zeke after several moments of tense silence. He could certainly understand why a man would get fixated with Cantara. "But why keep her in a cellar, half-starved?"

"That's what we're hoping your wife will be able to tell us, when she regains her memory. She might have information about people who visited Salim that will be useful to us."

"You're assuming she will regain her memory," Zeke pointed out.

"We sure as hell hope so," Pool replied. He had been very quiet during this exchange. Unusually so. Raoul wondered why.

"She only wanted to bring the warring factions together. She was no threat to anyone. We knew a lot of people wouldn't appreciate her intervention," Raoul said. "But we never figured some sick fuck would lock her away to satisfy his crazy obsession." He ran both hands through his hair. "Still, all that matters for now is that she's coming home. What do we know about her condition?"

It was Agent Parker who answered. "I won't sugar coat this," he said. "She had a severe skull fracture, probably caused by that fall you saw on video."

The muscle in Raoul's jaw flexed and hardened. "You think that caused her amnesia?"

Parker shrugged. "It's possible. Or it could be she was so traumatized that her mind closed down. I've seen it happen before. It's a natural defense mechanism."

"Yet she remembers our names," Zeke pointed out.

"She wasn't traumatized by you guys." Parker looked uncomfortable. "She was in a bad way physically when they picked her up. They've been concentrating on rehydrating her and getting some liquid nutrition into her. She's being sedated for the flight back here. Once she's here, we'll get her the best of care and talk to her when she's in a fit state to be interviewed."

"Ain't gonna happen," Raoul replied decisively. "She's coming home with us."

"Now hang on just one goddamned minute," Pool said. "We can give her the best of everything."

Raoul glowered at him. "You've already done more than enough. We are no longer soldiers, so you don't get to give us orders. Cantara is my wife. My responsibility." He fixed each man in turn with a steely look. "Discussion closed."

"Just as hot-headed as ever," Pool muttered. "But let me remind you that your wife was on official US government business when she was taken. She needs to be debriefed."

"She will be," Raoul said, glowering right back at the man he still blamed for Cantara's capture. "When she's well enough."

"You're on thin ice, Pool," Zeke added. "And in no position to lay down the law."

"Fortunately for you, our focus is on Cantara right now." Raoul scowled at Pool.

"Flight's on final, Colonel," a female adjacent said, poking her head around the door.

Raoul and Zeke jumped to their feet and shared a strained, anxious look. This was it. The time had come to welcome their baby home and Raoul couldn't remember the last time he had felt more nervous.

* * * *

Cantara felt as though she was floating. Or flying. There was a constant thrum that had nothing to do with the pains inside her head that she had learned to live with. Something was different. She didn't feel hungry, or thirsty. Nor was she too hot. Too cold. Too frightened to think. But everything inside her head was a haze. There was something she had to do. Something that was vitally important. But she was so damned tired, so comfortable for the first time for what felt like forever, that it took too much effort to try and think what it was. Whenever she had an inkling, it slipped away again like an elusive wraith.

There was a man on the periphery of her vision. Two men. One had intelligent gray eyes and dark hair that framed a rugged face. Those eyes softened when they looked at her, making her feel important, cherished. She liked it when that man stayed in her sketchy thoughts. She liked it even better when he was joined by another man with a swarthy complexion and piercing blue eyes.

Raoul. Why did that name spin through her vacant mind as though on a continuous loop? Why did she find it so comforting? And who or what was Ze?

"Shush, honey, keep still. You're awake, I see."

A cool hand touched her brow. A calm voice…well, calmed her. "Where am I?"

"In an airplane, sweetheart," the voice replied. "You will soon be home. Don't thrash about now. You'll dislodge the drip."

She glanced at her hand and saw a needle taped to the back of it, dripping liquid into a vein. She didn't want anything foreign pumped into her, but was too weak to object. It felt as though she was lying between crisp cotton sheets. She must be dreaming, imagining the calm voice and cool touch. And yet it all seemed so real. She felt clean, too.

"Sit up, honey, and we'll brush your hair." A button was pushed and the bed she was lying on slowly rose up so she was in a sitting position. "You need to look your best for your husband." *Husband?* "He's gonna be that glad to see you after all this time."

She felt a brush being gently pulled through her hair and ran a few strands of it through her own fingers. It was soft to the touch, untangled and smelled clean. When did she last have clean hair? Why was everyone being nice to her all of a sudden? And why was she in a plane? Cantara felt frightened and bewildered, but oddly reassured. She allowed whoever it was to brush her hair, wondering where home was and how she could have a husband and not know it.

"Here we go."

Someone removed the needle from her hand and fixed a seatbelt around her. The next thing she knew, the wheels of the plane she had been told she was in touched the tarmac with barely a bump. Nervousness gripped her as the plane taxied for a long time before coming to a stop.

The door was opened, but before anyone could help her to unfasten her belt, she was conscious of two men bounding onto the plane. She instinctively flinched. Men rushing up to her meant trouble. Pain. Always so much pain, such deprivation.

"Hey, baby."

She glanced to one side and gasped. The man from inside her head, the one with the penetrating gray eyes and devastating smile, crouched beside her and gently took her hand. He ran long fingers down the length of hers, soothing, reassuring, as he choked on a sob. She tried to snatch her fingers away, knowing better than to be taken in by him, but couldn't seem to find the energy. His eyes were moist as he leaned forward and brushed his lips against hers. Her head screamed at her to take evasive action. He was trying to lull her into a false sense of security by invading her dream. Her dreams were all she had left. Now they had gotten into those, too, and she had nothing left to fight back with. Tired. She was so damned tired.

The fear that threatened her brain didn't make it as far as her heart and she remained stock still, no longer caring what they did to her. Cantara mumbled, thinking she recognized the spicy tang of the lips that played over hers. It was memories of that taste that had seen her through her ordeal.

What ordeal?

She turned her head in the other direction, overwhelmed by a torrent of feelings that were as alien as they were confusing. Her imaginary male friend with blue eyes was on her opposite side, playing with her other hand, leaning in to kiss her as well. His hair, long, black, and shiny, seemed too real to be a figment of her imagination, dislodging a fragmented memory somewhere in the recesses of her addled brain. She closed her eyes, expecting the vision to dissipate and to find herself back in her dank, dark cellar—cold, hungry, and afraid of every small noise.

She opened her eyes again and focused, first to one side and then the other. They were both still there. Could they be real? Was one of them the husband she was supposed to have? Why wasn't she fighting them, like she had fought another man over a period that stretched into infinity? They were both speaking at once, quietly, their voices soothing, reassuring. She wasn't frightened of them, which was reason enough to be afraid. They had found a clever way to try and trick her. Let them do their worst, she thought wearily. She had reached the end of her tether and had no fight left in her.

"Baby," the first man said, his voice a soothing caress. "Don't you know us?"

She had never heard his voice so clearly in her dreams before. He had to be real. The large hand still holding hers was warm flesh and blood, confirming the fact. Without knowing where it had come from, a name sprang to her lips.

"Raoul?" she asked dazedly, blinking to clear the fog that imprisoned her memories. "Ze?"

Chapter Seven

Raoul was on emotional overload. One glance at Zeke told him his buddy was similarly afflicted. Cantara had stubbornly clung to life during the unimaginable hell she'd been through these past three years, but had almost reached breaking point. Her mind was gone, her lovely body emaciated, her eyes blank, her hair lank, lusterless. She was terrified of her own shadow. But not of them. Raoul grasped that one positive aspect of her condition, repeatedly telling himself she still knew who they were. That had to mean there was hope for her.

Didn't it?

"We're gonna take you home and make you better, darlin'," Zeke told her, running his fingers across the contours of her face with infinite tenderness.

Cantara simply looked at him, as though searching his face for the right answer. It was devastating to see just how comprehensively her feisty spirit had been broken, and it was all he could do not to give way to sobs fuelled by a combination of relief and fury. He would concentrate on the relief, and on ensuring Cantara got the best possible care to aid her recovery, however complete it turned out to be. Revenge could come later. It was too late to revenge themselves against Salim. The selfish bastard had deprived them of that pleasure. But they could and would redouble their efforts to find the traitor, Levi. No rock would be left unturned.

EMTs bounded on the plane.

"We need to get her onto a gurney," one of them said.

At the sound of his voice, Cantara emerged from her near catatonic state and became very agitated. Her blank eyes blazed with fear and she tried to back away from the man's voice. Still strapped into her seat, she couldn't move.

"She's petrified of men," the female nurse who had accompanied her told Raoul. "You two are the only ones she hasn't shied away from."

"She'll be all right with us," the same EMT said.

"Not a chance," Raoul replied, scowling as he tried not to think about what Salim and God alone knew who else had put her through to reduce her to such a wretched state. He leaned over to unfasten Cantara's seat belt, moving slowly, being as unthreatening as he could. "Come on, darlin'. I'm gonna get us out of here. Will you let me do that?"

He waited for a response, wondering if his words had even registered with her. Eventually he was rewarded with an uncertain nod. Raoul wrapped one arm around her bony shoulders and slid the other beneath her butt, sweeping her effortlessly into his arms. Just by looking at her, he had been able to see how much weight she'd lost. Picking her up, feeling her bones protruding through her flesh, looking at her gaunt, sunken cheeks, was graphic confirmation of just how deprived of basic sustenance she had been. Salim sure had a strange way of showing his supposed love for her. Raoul wasn't ready yet to think of what other indignities she had been forced to endure.

He expected her to struggle against him when he lifted her from her seat. Instead she sighed, closed her eyes, wrapped her arms around his neck and rested her head against his shoulder. Raoul couldn't tell if she was relieved, or wearily resigned, but he could feel her heart beating way too fast as her fragile body pressed against his chest. He shared a worried glance with Zeke as all the other people crowding onto the plane shuffled in the confined space to get out of his way.

With Zeke holding Cantara's hand and whispering comforting words to her in his native Arapaho, Raoul carried her down the steps and back onto American soil for the first time in over three years.

"We have the wagon here," the EMT said, pointing to the waiting ambulance.

"No need."

"You can't walk…"

This guy was starting to irritate the fuck out of Raoul. He dealt him a look that discouraged further argument as he and Zeke set out to walk the short distance to the administrative building. Cantara had been cooped up in way too many confined spaces recently. She needed to breathe fresh air, and to…well, to something. Hell if Raoul knew what. Her listless state was killing him and he would never stop blaming himself for screwing up the operation that had seen Cantara captured. He should have listened to his gut and known it was a set-up. Except Cantara would have been taken even if he had. Once they'd left the Israeli compound there was nothing he could have done to change anything, thanks to that groveling coward, Levi. They already had Cantara and were on to Raoul and Zeke. It was all such a fucking mess, but he and Zeke had been too busy wallowing in self-pity to go looking for answers. If they had, then perhaps—no, don't go there. He glanced down at Cantara, thanking a God he no longer believed in for restoring her to them alive—in body, at any rate. For now she was his first, his only, priority.

He was pleased when, presumably because she felt the fresh air peppering her face, Cantara opened her eyes. But her gaze was unfocused and she was clearly disorientated.

"We're at Andrews Air Force base in Washington, DC," he told her. "You're back in America, darlin', and no one will ever hurt you again. I promise you."

She showed no reaction, as though she had heard too many false promises over the past three years to believe anything anyone said to her. But he wasn't *anyone* and she must trust him on a visceral level, or she wouldn't be so passive in his arms. Would she? Hell if Raoul knew. She was giving nothing away. She had retreated some place where he couldn't reach her, as though she had learned the value of silence.

"This way." The EMT was still fussing around them. "She needs to be checked out in the medical facility."

Raoul wanted to argue, but shut his mouth again. He desperately wanted to be alone with her and Zeke, but knew she needed the kind of care he was incapable of giving her. If she suffered any setbacks because he'd kept the professionals away from her, he really would never forgive himself.

Pool, Hassan, and Parker fell in with their procession the moment Raoul pushed through the doors.

"How is she?" Parker asked.

"Frightened of men," Zeke replied before Raoul could.

"Give us some space here," Raoul said, when Cantara opened her eyes again, obviously saw all the men peering at her, and started to quiver.

They dropped back a little, all but the bossy EMT, who directed Raoul to a private room that had been set up in the base hospital for Cantara. Raoul put her on the bed. Without saying a word she curled up in a fetal position, turned away from him, and appeared to fall asleep.

"She will still have sedative in her system," the EMT said as Raoul pulled the covers up to her chin. "The doctor will be here shortly. You wanna wait out…"

Their identical expressions that said *you have got to be kidding me* killed the guy's half-formed question. He swallowed and backed toward the door.

"Someone will be right with you," he said.

The door closed behind him and Raoul and Zeke were finally alone with the love of their lives. They sat, one on either side of her, holding her hands and watching her sleep, not speaking. There was nothing left to be said. It shattered Raoul's heart to see her so broken, so defeated, but whatever could be done for her, would be. If Uncle

Sam didn't pick up the check, he and Zeke would take care of it. All he needed to know was what her prognosis was and how soon they could take her home.

A female nurse came in and checked Cantara's vital signs. She didn't wake up, but didn't fight against the nurse, either. The poor baby was totally wiped out. The flight, presumably, plus the sedative they have given her beforehand, to say nothing of her ordeal, had taken it out of her. The nurse told them there was a vending machine down the hall, but neither of them needed anything to eat or drink. What they needed was answers.

A male doctor appeared about half an hour later.

"You're Washington and Orion."

It wasn't a question, so Raoul merely stuck out his hand. "Washington," he said.

"Orion," Zeke said, following suit.

"I'm Major Blackhurst," he said, shaking each of their hands in turn. "Your gal here has had quite a time of it." He flipped through her medical records on an iPad. Presumably they had been sent from the Israel facility where she'd been treated. "She was lucky to come through it all. She must have quite a strong determination to live."

"What can you tell us about her condition?" Raoul asked.

"She had a severely fractured skull, which is healed."

"Is that why she's lost her memory?" Zeke asked.

"Could be. Taking a hit to the head is a pretty common reason for short-term memory loss. But we don't know if Ms. Amari's memory loss is short term because we don't know how long she's been like this."

"She's been held captive in pretty primitive conditions," Raoul replied, grinding his jaw. "We have no idea yet what was done to her, but could her memory have closed down as part of her body's defense mechanism?"

Blackhurst nodded. "Quite possibly. She might well have retreated in on herself to distract herself from her circumstances. It happens. I've seen quite a few victims of domestic abuse who use that technique to get by. They separate mind from body and don't feel what's happening to the body because their minds are saying it's not happening to them."

"Fuck!" Zeke muttered.

"There again," Blackhurst said, "it could be the skull fracture that caused the problems with her memory."

"Are you saying she won't ever recover?" Zeke asked.

"There's a good chance that she will. I've been told she screamed the place down in Israel when male doctors tried to go anywhere near her. And yet she recognized you two and let you carry her from the plane. That's a very good sign. She knew your names as well, right?" Both men nodded. "Well then, I'm optimistic. I'm gonna run some tests. I'd like to keep her here for twenty-four hours, then you can take her home."

"We can?" Raoul had expected the military to make an almighty fuss about her leaving.

"Best place for her. Peace and quiet. Time for her body and mind to heal, away from stresses and strains and, most importantly of all, away from figures of authority asking inane questions she's in no fit state to answer." He flashed a brief grin. "Not that you heard that from me."

"Did someone speak?" Zeke asked, causing Raoul to crack the first smile he'd been able to manage since Cantara lost consciousness again.

"When she starts to feel better, should we encourage her to remember?" Raoul asked.

"I'm sure that posse of high-ranking officers pacing about outside would be delighted if you succeeded," the physician replied with a wry smile.

"It's not them we're thinking about. We want to know if it would be dangerous for her physiologically to remember details of her ordeal, or if it would be therapeutic."

Blackhurst shook his head. "Not my field. You're gonna either have to use your own judgment as she starts to heal and—"

"See if she wants to know."

"Yep. Or better yet, get her to see a shrink."

Raoul sniffed, always having been of the opinion that naval-gazers did more harm than good with their intrusive questions. "We'll have to see about that. What I was thinking is that we've got pictures of her family, her life, before she got involved with what she was doing. Happy times before her family was wiped out by a bomb."

"Ouch!" Blackhurst flinched. "She's not had a good time of it, has she?"

"No, she sure ain't, but my point is that she *was* happy, once. There are good memories inside her head, mixed in with all the shit. Should we show her pictures of those happy times?"

"Only if she asks and you think she can handle the truth." Blackhurst spread his hands. "Sorry not to be more specific, but head injuries, combined with what Ms. Amari has been through, are not an exact science. All I can tell you is that some people will make a complete recovery, others won't. I prescribe love and affection, peace and quiet."

"She'll get as much of that as she can handle," Raoul said on a serrated sigh.

"Good to know. I'll run those tests now, then I'll have a dietician stop by and give you advice on how to feed her up again slowly. The right sorts of things for her to eat, stuff like that. Remember, she's been deprived of proper nutrition during her captivity, so feeding her too much of the wrong things too quickly could do more harm than good."

"We appreciate your advice," Raoul said, liking the man.

"Sorry not to be able to tell you what you need to hear, but I don't believe in making false promises. I hear you have a top neurologist ready to look at her in Wyoming."

"Yes, we have," Zeke said.

"Well, he might be able to tell you more."

Agent Parker in particular kept pressing to have just a few minutes' talk with Cantara. Raoul flatly refused, and was ready to deck him when he suggested she wouldn't be able to return to Wyoming until she had been debriefed. Like anyone could stop him and Zeke walking out with her. He would like to see them try it. The mood he was in right now, it would be a useful way to channel his anger and endless self-recriminations.

A drip was again inserted in Cantara's hand to feed her while she slept. Raoul and Zeke slept in the room with her, taking it in turns to stretch out in the other bed. One of them was always awake to watch over her, just in case she opened her eyes and needed something. She didn't. She slept soundly and, seemingly, wasn't troubled by dreams. Both men were watching her when she blinked her eyes open at eight the following morning. She had slept for sixteen hours straight.

"Hey, babe." Raoul gently touched her pale cheek. "How do you feel?"

"Where am I?"

It was the first question she had asked. In fact, they were the first words she had spoken since saying their names on the plane the previous day.

"You're back in the States, darlin'," Raoul told her. "You're safe now."

"We've got you, honey," Zeke assured her. "We don't plan on ever letting you out of our sight ever again."

"I need the bathroom."

It broke Raoul's heart when she looked around, as though seeking a pot in which to relieve herself. Is that how she'd had to live all this time?

"We'll get you to the bathroom, honey," Raoul said, ringing the bell. "Let's see if we can get this drip disconnected first."

She lay passively in bed, staring blankly at the ceiling until a nurse answered the bell.

"Hey," she said brightly to Cantara. "You're awake."

"She needs the facilities," Zeke said.

"I'm sure she does. Can you help her with that?"

"We've got her," Raoul replied as the nurse efficiently disconnected the drip.

"How about some breakfast, sweetheart?" the nurse asked.

Cantara didn't appear to understand the question.

"Bring her something," Zeke said. "We'll help her with it."

"What about you guys?" the nurse asked. "I'm sure we could rustle up something for you as well. I guess you missed dinner."

Raoul couldn't remember the last time either of them had eaten. "Yeah, that would be good, thanks."

When the nurse left them, Zeke pulled back the covers. Raoul went to pick her up to carry her to the bathroom, but before he could do so, she swung her legs over the side of the bed and stood. Almost immediately her knees buckled, but the guys held back from helping her, sensing she needed to do this on her own. She placed a fisted hand on the bed and pushed herself upright again. Raoul suspected this was how she had gotten through her ordeal. She had used her iron will to overcome adversity and show her defiance, even if it had been at the expense of her sanity.

"It's this way, darlin'," Raoul said as she looked around her, bewildered again, as though she had forgotten what it was she needed to do.

She made no attempt to shake off his hand when he placed it on her elbow and slowly guided her in the right direction. He turned his back while she used the toilet, giving her some privacy, but remaining in the room in case he was needed. He was unsure if she knew just how intimate they had once been and that he had seen and touched every inch of her naked body—with his hands, his lips, his cock. He pushed aside such thoughts and shared a look with Zeke. She had finished what her body told her it needed to do. Now she appeared to be waiting for instructions. Zeke moved toward the shower and turned it on.

"Come on, babe. You'll feel better after you freshen up."

She stood passively while he removed the hospital gown she had slept in. Both men were hard pressed to hide their reaction when her body was revealed to them. She had bruises and abrasions all over it, her once full breasts had withered and her hip bones looked as though they were about to burst through her skin. At a healthy one-twenty when they had last seen her, she now couldn't weigh more than eighty pounds.

"You think she can shower alone?" Zeke asked.

"Hell if I know."

Raoul slowly removed his T-shirt, giving her plenty of time to see what he was doing and object if she felt so inclined. She looked at him, her eyes registered alarm, followed by a brief show of life, and then became blank again. She wasn't screaming, or showing agitation, so he stepped out of the rest of his clothing and led her toward the shower. She went with him as meekly as a lamb.

"She must feel safe with us," Zeke said. "Even if she doesn't understand why. I'm pretty sure she hasn't taken many showers since we last saw her, but I'm willing to bet she would have put up one hell of a fight if anyone tried to relieve her of her clothes."

"Yeah, most likely. Our gal never was the passive type."

Cantara stood beneath the shower, eyes closed, head thrown back as water cascaded over it, and allowed Raoul to soap her all over. He did so with infinite tenderness, eliciting a sigh from her that made him feel like a million dollars because he knew it was a sigh of pleasure. The first pleasure she had known in a very long time. He squirted shampoo onto her head and gently rubbed it in. Then he let the water wash the lather away and repeated the process. By the time he had finished, Zeke was there with towels. He wrapped one around her wet hair and enveloped her slender body with another large, white fluffy sheet.

"There you go, darlin'," he said, kissing her neck. "Now don't that feel better?"

She nodded, but seemed too confused to speak. Zeke gently towel dried her hair and brushed it out for her. A few basic items of clothing had been left in the room and Raoul helped her into a pair of panties and another enveloping dress that cover her from neck to ankle, long sleeves concealing her stick-thin arms.

"Thank you."

The sound of her voice took them both by surprise.

"You're entirely welcome, sweetheart," Raoul said, choked by emotion at her gratitude for such a small service.

"Oh, you look better." The nurse who came in with a full breakfast tray smiled at Cantara. "I expect you're in a hurry to go home."

"Home?" she echoed in a dazed tone.

"Come along, darlin'," Zeke said. "There's English tea here. We know you like that. And your favorite cereal. You think you can manage that?"

She shrugged, but made no objection when the guys spoon fed her breakfast to her. They did so slowly, taking bites of their own omelets in between, giving her digestive system a chance to handle an influx of food that was a damned sight richer than the slop she'd most likely been living on for three years.

By the time she had finished, the doctor called again with her sign-out papers, which Raoul dealt with. Parker and Pool tried to barge in, but Zeke blocked the door.

"Not now," he said, crossing his arms over his torso. They didn't have a prayer of getting past him, and both appeared to know it. "We'll let you know when you can talk to her."

"Come on, darlin'," Raoul said, helping her to stand. "Let's go home."

Chapter Eight

Cantara had forgotten how comforting it could be to feel safe, always supposing she had ever known. All she could remember was being angry, cold, hungry, and afraid. And having pains in her head. All the time, pains. Before that her life was a blur, occasionally interspersed by fleeting memories that were gone before she could reach out and capture them.

These two men made her feel safe because she instinctively understand they were the exception to the rule and meant her no harm. The men who had featured so prominently in her dreams were actually warm, caring flesh and blood. She had not imagined them, so she assumed she must have known them in her previous life, accounting for her willingness to trust them when she had learned the hard way that no men were to be trusted.

The men—Raoul and Zeke—had brought her to safety, washed and fed her, telling her repeatedly how relieved they were to see her, because it was evident they hadn't expected to. Cantara knew they were sincere. She had no idea how she could be so sure, so willing to put her faith in them. She just was. Perhaps that's why she had slept without dreaming, sensing they were there all the time, watching over her, wrapping her in the security of their compassion.

What happened after that? It was so hard to separate myth from reality, but she did remember being sandwiched between them in what felt like a limousine. How did she know it was a limo, or even what a limo was? Had she been in one before? Then they were definitely in an airplane—just the three of them. She was strapped into a seat of soft sumptuous leather, wide enough for two people, and the plane took to the air. Her two saviors were piloting it because, of course, they were heroes and heroes could do everything.

Once they were in the air, one or the other them sat with her the entire time, holding her hand, talking softly to her. She found their voices soothing, comforting, and knew it was okay to close her eyes because at last she had people to look out for her. She thought she must have been given something for the pains in her head because they were no longer there. The medication had made her sleepy. Or perhaps it was the food she had eaten. She wasn't used to eating much at all. Tea, she remembered drinking tea and the explosion of nutmeg and cinnamon she associated with Earl Grey bringing her taste buds back to life. It was too tiring to work it all out. Her mind was such a fog, but she fought against sleeping. It wasn't safe to sleep when men were around. They tried to do things to her. Things she didn't want them to do.

She jerked upright, away from the troubling images playing tricks with her mind, and cried out, disorientated, afraid again.

"It's okay, darlin'," said the soothing voice of the man she recognized as Zeke. "You were dreaming, is all. You're quite safe."

"Hmm."

"Come on, I've got you. Close your eyes again and we'll be home before you know it."

"Home?" She blinked. "I don't have a home."

"Oh, sweetheart, you *so* do."

Zeke's cool hand gently wiped her hot forehead. Instantly reassured by his touch, she snuggled back down beneath the blanket someone had lain across her, grateful to feel warm for once. She must have slept, but without panicking this time, and woke when the wheels of the plane bumped against tarmac.

"Here we are, sugar," Raoul said. "We're home."

She rubbed the sleep from her eyes with her knuckles. "I wish I could remember," she said, so quietly that she didn't think they would hear her.

"You will, honey," Zeke replied. "When your mind decides the time is right."

They helped her from her seat and down a few steps. Zeke disappeared and returned behind the wheel of an SUV. How did she know it was an SUV? Some memory stirred in the back of her brain. So many fragments of jumbled information rattled around inside her head and she had no idea where they came from. It was disorientating.

"Come on, sweetheart."

Raoul helped her into the back seat and slid in beside her. He buckled her seatbelt for her, then attended to his own and rested an arm along the back of the seat, bringing it to rest on her shoulders. He looked at her apprehensively, as though he thought she might fight him off. That was her first instinct, but the moment his fingers caressed the top of her arm with slow, lazy swirling movements, she relaxed. Something that felt so soothing couldn't possibly cause her any harm. Besides, she had no fight left in her. Whatever these two guardian angels had in mind for her, she had no energy to protest.

She looked out of the window as they sped down a busy highway, wondering where she was being taken. She didn't ask because for as long as she could recall she had refused to speak at all. It had infuriated her captor when she refused to speak to him, but talking was now an effort. Besides, even if they told her the truth, she would be none the wiser.

Everything seemed to move so fast. All the cars were travelling at breakneck speed, as though the people in them had somewhere important to be. Zeke turned their car off the highway onto a quieter road. It must be summertime. The sun was high in the sky, bathing green plains with its brilliant rays. Horses and cattle were making the most of the verdant grass, and there was a range of craggy mountains in the distance. The Rockies. Cantara frowned. How did she know that? She noticed lakes everywhere, torpid water speckled a dozen different shades of turquoise by the sun. It was so serene that she sensed tension drain out of her, and felt an immediate affinity with her surroundings. No one who lived in this sort of place would try to hurt her, would they?

"Wyoming," she said abruptly.

"You know where you are?" Raoul looked delighted, as though she had said something remarkable. "That's great, babe."

"How did I know that?"

"It's where we all planned to live together, darlin'," Zeke replied from behind the wheel. "Before...well before what happened."

What did happen? "Oh."

The car slowed. Zeke turned it between two tall gateposts and paused at an electronic gate. Cantara tensed. Electronic gates meant high security, meant lack of freedom.

"Relax, babe," Raoul said easily, gently squeezing her hand. "This is home and the gates are to keep out unwelcome visitors."

She glanced at a sign on one of the pillars and noticed the name of the place. It was simply called *Cantara.*

"That's my name," she breathed as the gates swung open and Zeke drove through them.

"We named the spread after you," Raoul told her. "The first thing we did when we bought it was to change its name."

"Oh," she said again.

She stared out the window as they drove for what seemed like forever along a private road on the ranch's land. There was neat post and rail fencing keeping some lovely horses inside different paddocks. It seemed neat and well organized and she saw no people at all. Only animals. Animals were good. She liked animals.

The vehicle came to a halt in front of a sprawling brick and timber ranch house with a wraparound porch. Raoul jumped from the car, leaned back in to unfasten her belt, and offered her his hand. She paused for a second, then slipped hers into it, reassured rather than apprehensive when his long fingers closed around her palm. He helped her from the car and swept her from the ground.

"Welcome home, darlin'," he said, dropping his head to cover her lips with his own. "We missed you more than you could possibly know."

"Now this place feels complete," Zeke added, grasping one of her hands as Raoul carried her into the house.

Raoul put her down in what was obviously the great room—the heart of the house, with stunning views over paddocks dotted with horses either grazing or chasing one another around.

"It's lovely," she said. "Very peaceful."

"Which is just what you need," Zeke said, sliding an arm around her waist and standing with her to admire the view. "See that paddock there?" He pointed. She followed the direction of his finger with her eyes and nodded. "Those are Arabians. I promised you that when we got this place I would buy you an Arabian mare." The arm circling her waist tightened. "And I kept my promise, even though I never thought the day would come when you'd get to ride her."

"I can ride?" she asked, blinking. "I seem to remember that I can, but…" She shook her head, frustrated because the ephemeral memory had already slipped away.

"You can ride, honey," Raoul assured her, coming up on her either side and touching her face. She didn't even flinch. Zeke was holding her waist, Raoul was touching her face, and she didn't appear to feel threatened. Remarkable. "And Zeke broke that beautiful gray Arabian especially for you, the one there that's prancing around, showing off because she's almost as beautiful as you are. She's just waiting for you to take her out as soon as you're well enough."

"Her name is Iesha," Zeke said. "I remember you telling me once you thought it was a pretty name."

"It is pretty, but I don't remember that. I wish I did."

"The doctor says not to try too hard and the memories will come back in time," Raoul told her.

"Will they?" Cantara wondered if she wanted them to. She knew bad things that gave her nightmares and pain had happened to her. Now she felt safe. Why not start her life anew from today?

"Sure they will." Raoul kissed her cheek. "But now, I'm gonna cook us something to eat and then I guess you'll want to sleep. You have a lot of adjustments to make."

"Yellow!" She jumped with excitement. "You promised me a yellow room."

They shared a glance and smiled simultaneously. "And we keep our promises," Raoul said. "Well, most of them," he added, scowling at some memory he didn't choose to share with her. "Come see for yourself."

He was like a little boy on Christmas morning, bursting with excitement as he took her hand and led her down a corridor. Zeke opened a door and she found herself in a huge room, painted sunshine yellow, with windows on three sides. A huge, very comfortable-looking bed dominated the room, and the lightwood furnishings and floral drapes were just what she would have chosen for herself. She gasped with delight.

"I saw a room like this, inside my head, when...I don't know when. But I saw it."

"We kept it for you, even though we thought you were..." Raoul shot Zeke a look and his words trailed off. "Well, we haven't been in here for a long time."

She wondered why not, but didn't ask. "Your clothes from before are in there," Raoul said, indicating the walk-in closet. "They'll be too big right now, but we can get you new things. And the bathroom's right through that door."

"Do you want to rest before supper?" Zeke asked. "You've been through a lot today."

"No, I want to stay with you all." She blinked, surprised by the spontaneous admission.

"Come on then, darlin'," Raoul said, holding out his hand. "You can sit in the other room, while we fix you a welcome home dinner."

* * * *

Zeke sat with Cantara while Raoul busied himself in the kitchen. She seemed distant, but less anxious than she had been, hopefully at ease with them here in the home they had built for her, never expecting her to occupy it. The yellow room had been made for the three of them to share. Neither he nor Raoul had set foot in it once the decorating and furnishing was done and they had filled it with Cantara's possessions. A shrine to the woman they loved and had let down when she'd needed them the most. Same went for Iesha. She was the perfect mare for Cantara—spirited, beautiful, and just a little wilful. Breaking the mare to saddle had somehow made Zeke feel closer to Cantara's spirit.

Now, against all the odds, they were blessed with the return of the woman herself. This time they would not fail her.

"Thanks, bud," Zeke said as Raoul handed him a beer and placed a cup of Earl Grey at Cantara's side. She looked at it for a protracted moment, as though wondering what she was supposed to do with it, and then smiled.

"Thank you, Raoul," she said in a soft, sultry voice that sounded as though it hadn't gotten much use over the past few years.

Raoul's smile was wider than the Mississippi. "It's entirely my pleasure, darlin'," he replied, briefly touching her face because, like Zeke, he could get enough of touching her.

"It's hard for me," she said, surprising Zeke by speaking without being asked a question. It was virtually the first time it had happened and caused Raoul to stop chopping vegetables and look up at her expectantly.

"What is, sugar?" Zeke asked, knowing full well what she would most likely say.

"Not being able to remember who I am. It's like someone has drawn a curtain through my mind. Occasionally it flaps open and I see glimpses of things."

"Like the yellow room?"

"Yes, like that."

"It was important to you, sugar. That's probably why. So was coming to live in Wyoming, and you remembered that name." Zeke paused. "And our names, too."

"I thought you weren't real," she said. "I kept seeing your faces but I thought I was dreaming again when you came to get me from that plane."

The pathos in her tone broke Zeke's heart. "We're real, sweetheart, and we're never gonna let you out of our sight again."

"I'm figuring you'll remember more and more real quick now," Raoul said from the kitchen as he supervised his grilled fish. "Every day you'll feel a little stronger, a little safer, and your mind will be ready to unlock itself."

She looked distressed. "But what if it doesn't?"

Zeke picked up her hand and kissed each of her fingers in turn. "Then we'll help you, sweet thing. Never doubt it for a moment."

"We've got a specialist coming to see you tomorrow," Raoul said. "I just spoke to his office and fixed it up. He doesn't usually make house calls, but for a special lady like you, he's willing to make an exception."

She tensed up. "Don't leave me alone with him."

"I already told you," Zeke said gently. "You never have to be alone again."

"But why can't I remember?" she asked, frowning. "Why do I know what some things are instinctively and yet I can't remember what happened last week?"

"You hurt your head," Zeke told her, because she didn't seem to know. "Bad bangs to the head sometimes cause memory problems."

"Oh, perhaps that's why I get so many headaches."

"You need to tell the doctor about those tomorrow," Zeke said. "He'll be able to help you, I expect."

"Yes, perhaps he will." She shared a protracted glance between them. "The lady on the plane told me I was going to meet my husband. Is one of you my husband?"

How to answer that one? "Would you like one of us to be?" Zeke countered cautiously.

"I think so," she replied after a long hesitation. "You make me feel safe, and I know I haven't felt safe in a long time, especially around men." She shook her head. "But I can't decide which of you I prefer."

"Why not settle for us both?" Raoul asked, blowing her a kiss from the open kitchen area.

Her eyes widened and Zeke was encouraged to see them light up, albeit briefly. "Is that allowed?"

Both men threw back their heads and laughed. "Oh yeah, babe," Raoul replied for them both. "It's definitely allowed, but as far as the rest of the world's concerned, you're married to me. Is that okay with you?"

"Yes, I think so."

"Well, that's real good. Now come on you two, dinner's ready."

Cantara fed herself this time, picking at her salad and the grilled fillets of fish Raoul had prepared, along with tiny potatoes and green beans. She cleared her plate of the small portion Raoul had given her.

"That was nice," she said. "Thank you."

"Seeing you eat it all is thanks enough," Raoul said, clearing away the dishes. "And it just so happens that I have some raspberry ice cream. Your favorite."

She gave him a blank stare. "Is it?"

"You tell us," Zeke replied, dishing some up and placing it in front of her.

She picked up the spoon, took a little of the frozen dessert into her mouth and savored it slowly. "Hmm, it tastes real good, but I don't remember having it before."

Shit, Zeke thought. She used to eat it all the time.

"You can have more next time," Raoul promised her. "Have to get you used to this stuff again slowly or your insides will protest."

"Why?" she asked with another of her bewildered looks.

"Don't worry about it, sweet thing," Raoul replied, dropping a gentle kiss on her brow. "Just concentrate on getting better one day at a time."

She stifled a yawn with the back of her hand.

"Come on, darlin'," Zeke said, standing and taking her hand to pull her to her feet. "It's getting dark and you're beat. It's time for you to get some rest."

Together Zeke and Raoul did what they had never imagined they would get to do, and got the love of their life ready for bed in the home they had created for her. Her eyes were dropping by the time they'd helped her to wash, brush out her hair and slip into a silk nightgown that Raoul had bought for her in a previous life. It hung off her emaciated frame, but she seemed to find the touch of the silk against her skin soothing. Zeke pulled back the covers and Raoul lifted her into the middle of the huge bed—a bed which they had given up all hope of ever sharing with her.

Now that hope had been resurrected—but it wouldn't happen tonight. She needed to get used to being back in civilization first. She needed time to heal. Each man kissed her brow as Zeke pulled the covers up to her chin.

"Sleep well, darlin'," Raoul said. "We're both right down the hall. Just call if you need anything and we'll come running. We'll leave the door slightly open so we can hear you if you want us. Is that all right?"

She mumbled something incoherent and curled into a ball on her left side. Zeke and Raoul waited until her breathing became slow and even and they were pretty sure she was asleep. The doctor had given them sleeping pills for her but both men were against the idea of her taking them unless absolutely necessary. They were here to help her through her neurosis. She didn't need chemical additives messing with her already messed-up mind.

They ought to leave her but lingered a little longer, drinking in the sight of her. In repose, with the covers over her thin body, she looked almost like the Cantara of old. Except she would never be that person again. Part of Zeke thought it would be better if her memory didn't come back, but he also knew that unless she faced her demons, she would never be free of the fears that gripped her.

"What do you make of her?" Zeke asked as they crept away and sat together in the great room, sipping beers straight from the bottles.

"I think there's a good chance she'll get her memory back," Raoul replied. "Odd things are occurring to her already. Whether that will be a good thing or not, is another matter."

"Yeah, I hear you." Zeke felt a murderous rage streak through him. "When I see how cowed she now is, how petrified of men, it makes me wanna commit a few murders of my own."

"Then we're on the same page." Raoul's expression was set in stone. "We know who took her, and why. He's dead so there's nothing we can do about him. What we *can* do is track down Levi and make him regret the day he was born for what he put her through."

"I still find it hard to believe that he did it," Zeke said, shaking his head. "I thought he was as straight as a die."

Raoul shrugged. "Just goes to show. A fool who can't control his cock can land up in all sorts of shit. He should have known better than to get caught in a honey trap. Once that happened, he belonged to the guys who trapped him."

"Yeah, I guess." Zeke stretched his arms above his head and grinned. "We have her back, man. That's all that counts. I still can't believe it. We'll get her fit again physically, get some meat back on her bones, and hopefully the rest will follow."

"We'll know more tomorrow after..." A bloodcurdling scream had them both leaping to their feet. "What the fuck!"

They ran to Cantara's room and switched on the lights. She was thrashing about in the huge bed, her body bathed in perspiration, the silk nightgown twisted in knots around her. But it was her face that worried them the most. She was whiter than the sheets she had kicked aside, and the terror in her eyes tore at their heartstrings. Even though her eyes were wide, she was clearly still asleep, gripped by a nightmare.

"Cantara," Raoul said in a firm yet gentle voice. "Honey, can you hear me?"

He touched her arm and she flinched like he had struck her. She tried to pummel him with her fists, possessed of superhuman strength.

"Get off of me!" she screamed in Arabic. "I don't want to."

"Cantara, wake up." Raoul lightly tapped the side of her face. Zeke flinched, knowing he would have hated doing it. Seeing her in the grip of such unmitigated horror made it necessary. "Come on, darlin', it's just a dream."

Her body abruptly stopped trembling and she quit fighting him. Her eyes alighted upon him and she looked confused.

"You were having a bad dream," Raoul said gently, stroking the hair away from her face. "That's all it was."

"Don't leave me," she said, trembling. "Please don't leave me here alone."

Zeke and Raoul shared a look, shed their clothes in seconds and climbed into the bed, one on either side of her. Zeke took her hand as Cantara rested her head on Raoul's shoulder. She sighed just once and mumbled something that sounded like *much better.*

"We won't ever leave you, darlin'," Zeke assured her. "We'll always be here for you."

"Hmm."

She seemed reassured and within seconds she was sound asleep again. This time she slept through the night without once stirring.

* * * *

Cantara woke feeling rested, stronger. Of course, that might have had something to do with the two hunky bodies that had surrounded her throughout the night. She had drawn from solid protectiveness that felt so non-threatening that she mentally ceded responsibility for her wellbeing to them. The relief was palpable—as though a huge weight had been lifted from her shoulders.

She stretched and flung one arm carelessly to the side. An empty side. Her eyes flew open. They had left her. They'd promised they wouldn't. Didn't they realize how badly she needed them?

"Hey, easy baby," said a voice from her other side.

She turned to see Raoul, leaning up on one elbow, his eyes alight with an unfathomable emotion as he watched her.

"I thought…I thought you had gone, that I'd dreamed it all." Panic she was unable to conceal gripped her. "I was back in—"

"Shush. We won't ever leave you again." He brushed her hair away from her forehead with a delicate touch, lowered his head and gently covered his lips with his own. "Zeke has gone to make us some breakfast, is all."

"What time is it?"

"Eight in the morning. You slept for twelve hours, apart from one brief nightmare."

"I don't usually sleep at all." She frowned. "Well, I don't think I do."

"Well, I'm glad you feel secure enough to sleep here in your yellow room, darlin'." He slipped an arm around her shoulders and pulled her against him. "I am so goddamned relieved to have you back, Cantara." His shoulders shook and tears leak from the corners of his eyes. He was actually crying. Her beautiful, tough hunk of a husband who didn't look as though anything could scare him was reduced to tears because he had missed her, and because he seemed to feel guilty about her ending up wherever it was she'd been to. "I'm so sorry I failed you."

"I'm sure you didn't fail me." She snuggled up to the rock hard wall of warmth and safety that was his chest, anxious to reassure. "I think I must be pretty strong-willed."

Raoul chuckled through his emotional turmoil. "Well, there is that."

"You need to tell me what happened. It might help me remember, and absolve you from guilt."

"We will, honey. But not yet. You need time to readjust before you relive your nightmares."

"Whatever you think best."

He smiled that meltingly gentle smile of his that so got to her and cupped her chin in his long fingers. "What I think best is having you here in this bed with us. I never thought it was gonna happen."

She could feel something pressing against her thigh. Something hard. Yea gods, he had an erection! She panicked and jerked out of his arms. Did he want what the other one wanted from her—the one who had frightened her, hurt her? Wasn't that what all men wanted, even the civilized ones like Raoul? Nice try, but she was onto him.

"Sorry," he said, looking embarrassed. "It's just the way you make me feel. Ignore it. It'll go away on its own."

"Raoul…I can't…I don't think I want to—"

"Listen to me, darlin'," he said, holding her by the shoulders and looking intently into her eyes. "You've had one hell of a time. We can't begin to imagine what you've been through." *Nor could she, that was the problem. It would help if she could remember.* "But you're safe now, and no one's gonna make you do anything you don't want to. Trust me on this."

"I do trust you, Raoul," she said, relaxing back against him. "But it's confusing, not knowing who I am or what I've done, and being afraid of my own shadow. I don't feel as though I'm the sort of person who scares easily, which makes it that much more frustrating."

"Shush, I know." He placed a finger against her lips and sent her another of his devastating smiles. It lit up his features, transforming his face from merely handsome to drop-dead gorgeous. "But we have all the time in the world now to make you better. You'll remember when you're ready to."

Zeke joined them at that point, carrying a tray bearing their breakfast. He was wearing a ratty pair of cut-off jeans and, far as Cantara could tell, not a whole lot else. She might still be feeling weak, but not so weak that she couldn't appreciate his sculpted torso, his rippling muscles and graceful coordination. He and Raoul were impossibly good looking and self-assured, but there the similarities ended. Zeke was part Arapaho. She sat a little straighter as she recalled him telling her that yesterday.

"What is it, babe?" Raoul asked.

"I can remember every single thing about yesterday," she said dazedly. "I can remember bits about flying with a nurse on a plane, too. It felt like we flew a long way and then you and Zeke came to take me from that plane. That memory is spasmodic but I remember yesterday in its entirety. I remember everything since you guys came to get me." She looked from one to the other of them expectantly. "Am I getting my memory back, or is my life starting from yesterday?"

"I don't know, darlin'," Zeke said, putting the tray down on a table beside the bed. "But it must be a good thing that you remember everything since we picked you up. We'll ask the neurologist when he comes later today."

She ate fruit and yogurt and drank more Earl Grey. Then the guys asked her if she wanted to shower and dress, or did she want to see the doctor in bed?

"No, I want to get up."

She pushed the covers aside and stood up, pleased that her knees didn't give out beneath her this time. The straps of the nightgown she was wearing slid down her arms and the entire garment pooled at her feet. They both stared at her in her nudity, but Cantara felt no necessity to cover herself. She didn't know what to make of their expressions and so simply walked to the bathroom, trying not to show how much she didn't want them to be disappointed by what they saw. She was too thin, her body a mass of bruises and scars that she had no recollection of acquiring.

But she was alive.

Cantara set the shower running and stood beneath the jets for a long time, soaping herself thoroughly and using the fragrant shampoo she found in the stall to wash her hair. Raoul had washed it for her the previous day but now that she could afford the luxury of washing herself as often as she liked, she would do precisely that. Eventually, with a lot of luck, she would feel clean again.

She walked back into the bedroom with towels wrapped around her body and hair. Both guys were still there, presumably in case she needed their help. She was glad to prove to herself that she didn't.

"Better?" Zeke asked.

"Much, thanks."

Raoul blew her a kiss. "Let me help you find something to wear, darlin'."

He levered himself athletically from the bed, not seeming to mind that he was stark naked. In all honesty, Cantara didn't mind either. He was a sight to behold and she looked her fill, thinking she had good taste in husbands. Powerful muscles shifted and flexed as he moved across the room with catlike grace, sending her a devastating smile that she reacted to somewhere deep within her core. It was as though her body was emerging from a deep trauma and her feminine side was reacting to the attentions of a handsome man in just the way nature intended. She was glad that at least one part of her seemed to be in good working order.

She followed Raoul into her closet. He handed her a pretty pair of panties, the sight of which set off a fleeting memory.

"I bought them for you just after we married," he explained in response to her confusion. "There's a bra to match but you won't need that until we've put some weight back on those pretty little tits of yours."

He fleetingly touched one of the breasts in question and Cantara felt a sharp, tangible need rip through her. She gasped, sending Raoul a questioning glance. He chuckled, seemingly pleased by her response.

"Zeke and I have always been able to turn your lights on with just a touch," he told her. "Seems nothing has changed."

Both of them? "You mean, you, me, *and* Zeke?"

"It will all become clear. Sorry, sweetheart, I shouldn't have said anything to confuse you more than you already are."

He helped her into a cozy sweatshirt and comfortable cotton pants with an elasticated waist that prevented them from falling straight back down again. She thrust her feet into the slippers Raoul found for her, then went back to the bathroom and towel-dried her hair.

By the time she emerged into the great room, she heard the guys talking to someone. She panicked, and went to turn back to the yellow room—her safe haven.

"Hey, sweetheart." Raoul held out a hand and she instinctively slipped hers into it. "This is Dr. Sanford. He's the best man in the area to look after you. Will you let him do that?"

"Don't leave me," Cantara replied, panic building inside her.

"Not for a second," Zeke assured her, taking her other hand and leading her to the seats they had occupied the night before.

Cantara sat between her two guys, feeling apprehensive of the stranger with kind eyes, but mildly euphoric because she *could* remember sitting there before.

"Hello, Cantara," Dr. Sanford said in a gentle, non-threatening voice. "I hear you've had quite a time of it. Welcome home."

* * * *

Sanford already had copies of Cantara's medical records from the base hospital at Andrews. He had told Raoul and Zeke he was especially interested in their girl's condition. Trauma associated with captivity was a specialty of his. That was undoubtedly why such an eminent consultant had agreed to make a house call. He spent over an hour with Cantara, gently asking questions that she mostly couldn't answer. She was tense at first, but when it became apparent that Sanford meant her no harm, she gradually relaxed. But not to the extent that she was prepared to let go of Raoul's hand. She clutched it so tightly during the entire hour that she was in danger of cutting off the blood flow to his fingers.

"Thank you, Cantara," Sanford said when he stood up to leave. "It's been a pleasure meeting you and I hope you start feeling better real soon."

"Stay with Zeke a moment, babe," Raoul said, ensuring Zeke had firm hold of her other hand before he extracted his from her grasp. He got up and moved out of ear shot with Sanford.

"What's your opinion?" he asked anxiously.

"The memory loss was originally attributable to the fractured skull," he replied. "Then she found herself in such a traumatic situation that her mind couldn't handle it and closed down. There's no reason why the memories shouldn't come back, but she'll need a lot of support to get through them when they do."

"She'll get it. Count on that."

"I know she will."

"Should we encourage her to remember, or is she better off not knowing?"

"Unfortunately there are no hard and fast rules in these cases. I know that's not what you want to hear, but only Cantara can know what's right for her. My advice is, if she asks and you think she's strong enough to take it, then show her pictures of her past, tell her things. Drop the odd comment into conversations and see how she reacts. You know her better than anyone, so you're the best person to judge what she can and can't handle." Sanford handed him a card. "My business and personal numbers are on there. I'm very interested in Cantara's recovery."

"You think she *will* recover?" Raoul jumped on the suggestion.

"I think there's every chance." Sanford flashed a professional smile. "She's a tough young lady. And, in case you're blaming yourself, it's my belief that thoughts of you got her through her ordeal. She wouldn't have remembered your names otherwise."

"Thank you for that," Raoul said, offering the consultant his hand as he walked him to the door. "It helps a lot."

Chapter Nine

Over the next four weeks, Cantara's rate of progress exceeded Raoul's most ambitious expectations. Each day they saw small improvements in her. Her appetite returned, so did her strength. She gained a little weight, looked a little less gaunt, and the shadows lifted from her eyes. Her bruises had gone, her cuts healed and her scars began to fade. The physical ones, anyway. She walked longer distances with the two of them each day and got to know Iesha. The mare quickly caught on to the fact that Cantara was a soft touch and was waiting at the railings every morning for the treat Cantara took her.

"That mare is precocious," Zeke declared, chuckling.

"She is magnificent," Cantara replied defensively, smoothing her sleek neck and kissing her soft muzzle.

"Whatever you say works for me," Raoul said. If she said the moon was made of cheese, who was he to argue?

She met Mark and Karl and didn't seem afraid of them, which was encouraging. The guys had taken over the day to day running of the Agency while Raoul and Zeke devoted themselves exclusively to Cantara's recovery. Significantly, she remembered more and more snippets, and asked more questions about what had happened to her. But her memories were still patchy and the guys had decided she wasn't strong enough to hear the complete truth just yet.

"It's very early days," Sanford told Raoul during one of their many telephone consultations. "She's doing way better than I would have expected at this stage. Just don't push her too hard."

A significant breakthrough came when Cantara had been in Wyoming for almost three weeks. They had fallen into the routine of Zeke helping Cantara to bed while Raoul tidied up the day's business, answering any queries Mark and Karl couldn't handle. That gave Cantara a bit of time alone with Zeke. Raoul made it to bed in time to kiss her goodnight, before her eyes fluttered to a close and she snuggled up between them. She occasionally woke in a sweaty panic but they had taken to leaving a low light burning in the room, so she knew immediately where she was. That she was safe. The nightmares appeared to come less and less frequently after that.

In the mornings it was Raoul's turn to be alone with her while Zeke fixed breakfast. Raoul loved waking before she did, just so he could watch her sleeping and observe the small changes that had occurred in her since the previous day. No one would ever convince Raoul that he didn't notice each and every one of them, no matter how insignificant.

This morning, Cantara turned the tables on him. He woke to find her leaning up on an elbow, watching him.

"Hey, you applying for my job?" he asked, leaning up for a kiss.

She returned that kiss with considerable enthusiasm. Up until now she had been wary of excess physical contact, and so he and Zeke had kept their kisses chaste. But this morning that didn't seem to be enough for her. Her lips parted beneath his in an invitation that was simply too tempting for Raoul to resist. He had been burning with desire ever since her return, his frustration growing daily more acute as he yearned to exorcise her demons in a manner he knew the Cantara of old would have embraced with enthusiasm. He had been able to keep his instincts in check all the time she had been passive, but asking him not to follow up the messages she was now sending him—intentionally or otherwise—was too much.

With a groan, Raoul plundered her mouth with his tongue, savoring the sweet taste of her. With their lips still fused Raoul sat up, gathered her onto his lap and closed his arms possessively around her as he deepened the kiss. Her lips were soft and warm beneath his as Raoul kissed her like it was an Olympic sport and he a contender for the gold medal. He invested his heart and soul into that kiss, telling her without the need for words just how comprehensively he loved her, and how his heart had shattered to smithereens when he had thought she was dead. Her arms worked their way around his neck and her fingers tangled with his hair, just the way they used to. Did she remember that, or was her action instinctive?

"Baby," he said, breaking the kiss, breathless and aroused. "We need to stop this right now, while I still can."

"What if I don't want to stop?" she asked, canting her head flirtatiously.

"I don't want to take advantage."

She chuckled, a throaty, confident sound he hadn't heard her emit since her return and which filled Raoul with joy. "You've been teasing me with one of these every morning since I got home." She reached beneath her butt to flick at his hard-on. "It's about time you made good on your promise."

"Nothing would give me greater pleasure, you have no idea, but—"

"We did things together, didn't we? You, me and Zeke."

"You remember that?"

"Flashes. I saw the picture by your computer the other day and knew it was Las Vegas. We had just gotten married and the three of us didn't leave the hotel room for two whole days after that."

"That's right." Raoul flashed a warm smile. "And we still couldn't get enough of you."

"I want that again," she said softly. "I need to start living again, Raoul. I feel so much stronger. I need to get my life back."

Raoul knew this was a defining moment. The first time she had made demands of any kind. "So, you only want me for my body?" he teased.

"Don't pretend it's not mutual, Washington," she said, biting her lip to quell a giggle. Raoul wanted to tell her not to. Hearing his wife giggle uninhibitedly would kick start his healing process, too. "That big old cock of yours gives you away."

"And it's all yours, if you still want it, darlin'," he said, fixing her with a smoldering smile. "Always has been, and always will be."

It filled Raoul's heart with joy to see her eyes darken with desire. "Then it must be my lucky day," she said in a husky voice.

"I don't know what you remember about the games you used to play with Zeke and me," he said, rolling her off his thighs and eliciting a squeal from her as he tumbled her onto her back. Raoul's gaze roved over her rapidly recovering body as, hair fanned out beneath her, she treated him to the sultry smile that had haunted his dreams these past three years. "We'll be happy to remind you, once you're strong enough. But right now, I'm gonna take this real gentle, and you have to promise to tell me if I hurt you."

"You won't," she replied, tracing the curve of his face with the tips of her fingers. "I know you won't, because you love me."

"More than you can possibly know. Way more. I'm a one woman guy, Cantara, and you're that one woman, darlin'."

He lowered his head to claim her lips as his fingers gently explored the contours of her body, which were slowly taking shape again. Her tits were as sensitive as ever. She proved it by groaning around their fused lips as he softly pinched a solidified nipple.

"You like that, sweetheart?" he asked, breaking the kiss because he needed to hear her say it.

"Yes," she replied breathlessly. "I like everything you do to me. I remembered that when I woke up this morning, but I think subconsciously I knew it before then. That's why I feel so safe with you and Zeke, and now that I've admitted it, I'm not afraid for you to touch me anymore."

"I'm so very glad you feel that way, sweetheart." Her admission earned her another searing kiss. "You used to like this, too. A lot."

He started at her neck, gently nipping and lapping his way to the pulse beating at the base of her throat. He worked his way methodically downwards, cupping one of her small breasts and giving the nipple the attention it cried out for by sucking it into his mouth. She gasped as he kissed a trail down to her abdomen, his tongue swirling, tantalizing and teasing.

"I still do like it." She gasped. "You know all the right places to agitate."

"Is that right?"

"Hmm."

"We only just got started. We haven't got to the best part yet."

He continued on down to her pussy, pushed her legs apart, knelt between them, and bent to feast on her nub. She cried out, throaty little gasps of pleasure he remembered as being so uniquely her. She tasted so goddamned sweet, was just as responsive as she had always been. Raoul was dangerously out of control, his cock throbbing so hard that he could easily shoot his load then and there. That couldn't be allowed to happen. This one was for her.

All for her.

He sat back on his haunches, taking a moment to rein himself in, and examined her face for signs of distress. Her eyes were closed and she seemed totally with the program. Reassured, Raoul slid a couple of fingers into her cunt, slick with her juices, and rubbed the pad of his thumb over her clit.

"Raoul!"

Her eyes flew open and she looked at him with a wild entreaty that definitely had no basis in anxiety. He chuckled and added a third finger.

"That what you need?"

"No, I want you."

"All in good time, darlin'. All in good time. It's a sin to rush these things."

He increased the pressure of his thumb, and pushed his fingers a little deeper into her tight pussy. She cried out, bucked her hips against his hand, and exploded. Raoul watched her face as she rode her orgasm, loving the fact that she could be so uninhibited so soon after her ordeal. Loving it even more that the suggestion had been hers.

"Better?" he asked when she came back down to earth and opened her eyes again.

"Hmm." She squirmed beneath him. "Was that the appetizer?"

Raoul laughed aloud. "Dr. Sanford didn't actually prescribe this treatment, but perhaps he should have done. We shall look upon it as medicinal and administer regular doses. How does that sound, babe?"

"Like heaven."

Raoul leaned over her, supporting his weight on his forearms. Not a great fan of vanilla sex, right now it had never seemed more appealing. He parted her creamy folds and slid the tip of his throbbing cock into her, just an inch or two, still not totally convinced she was ready for this. Too far gone to deny her. He ached with a need Cantara could spend the rest of her life satiating—for him and for Zeke.

Part of him wished his buddy could have been there when Cantara took this big step forward on the path to recovery, both physical and carnal. Another part of him figured both of them at once would be too much for her when she was still so fragile. Zeke would get his, now she was back in the saddle, just so long as she didn't react aversely to what they were about to do. He still didn't know if she'd been forced to have sex with that bastard Salim. Raoul ground his jaw at the prospect, not wanting to know if she had been, but figured she needed to face it sooner or later. *Make that later.*

He was reassured when Cantara wrapped her legs around his waist and locked them at the ankles, as though afraid he might change his mind. Like he could! She was so damned tight—way tighter than he recalled, but perhaps it was more to do with the extent of his tumescence. He tried to work his way into her gently, but his feisty Cantara was having none of it. She thrust her pelvis upwards to meet his next thrust and before he knew it he was completely sheathed in her enveloping warmth. They groaned in unison and, satisfied that she was comfortable, Raoul picked up the pace.

"You used to spank me," she said on a breathless sigh.

"Yeah, and you loved it."

"Will you do that again?"

"I'll do whatever you want me to, sweetness, but not too fast. We need to build up to these things."

"Sure we do."

There was a mischievous light in her eye as she thrust against him with increased force, gyrating her hips as she did so, creating an almost unbearably intoxicating friction between them. She clenched the muscles in her pussy against his length, adding to his agony. Straining to explode, Raoul couldn't let that happen yet. She needed to come first, and come hard. She'd damn well earned the right. He increased the pace and ferocity of his thrusts, watching her for signs of distress that didn't materialize. Instead her cute little needy moans increased in volume and intensity by the second.

"That's it, darlin'. Now we're really fucking. You've got everything I can give you, Cantara, honey. God, I never dreamed I'd get a second chance with you. I love you so damned much it hurts. I'm never gonna let you out of my sight again. Get used to it."

"I love it that you're so protective."

"Yeah," he groaned, breathless from the flickering heat building deep inside of him. "But do you love me, darlin'? Do you forgive me?"

"I love you, and I love Zeke." Her fingers clawed at his back. "Don't care if that sounds greedy. As to forgiving, there's nothing *to* forgive, unless you count the fact that you're deliberately teasing me when you know I need to come real bad."

He chuckled. "Okay, darlin', let's do this together."

"Raoul! Oh my God, I…"

Cantara had no breath left to finish her sentence. Raoul gloried in the feel of her tightening muscles around his throbbing cock, drank in her expression of astounded ecstasy as she thrashed her head from side to side and absorbed her orgasm like a woman with a point to prove to herself. A woman who definitely felt ready to embrace life again. Her pleasure was Raoul's undoing. His dwindling self-control evaporated and with a growl of fierce possessiveness he shot his load deep inside the woman he had loved since the moment he set eyes on her. The woman whom he had thought was lost to him forever.

Against all the odds, they had been granted a second chance and this time Raoul and Zeke wouldn't be taking any risks when it came to Cantara's welfare.

* * * *

Zeke whistled tunelessly as he carried the breakfast tray toward the yellow room, pleased with the simple domesticity of the task. Even more pleased with Cantara's progress. The shell of the woman who had returned to them was blossoming into the wild and beautiful creature who had haunted Zeke's dreams. Curiosity was replacing Cantara's mental inertia. She asked more and more questions about their past, about what had happened to her, and Zeke was confident she would gradually remember everything for herself. Something small and insignificant would open the floodgates, and there it would all be. So would Raoul and Zeke, ready to help her through the traumatic aftermath.

Sanford was delighted with her progress. Now that he knew her better he agreed she was the sort of person who needed to remember, rather than bury the past. Only then would she be truly free to start living again. Once she had remembered, he and Raoul could concentrate on finding that sniveling bastard Levi and giving him what he had coming. A man who betrayed his country's interests in order to save his own miserable hide was the worst kind of coward, and Raoul and Zeke would know no peace until he was held to account.

They had Cantara back, it was true, but that was no thanks to Levi. They lived with daily evidence of the horrors she'd suffered because of him—her haunted expression, her injuries, the nightmares, the long stretches of time she spent staring vacantly into space—to say nothing of the loss of her memory and three of the best years of her life.

And theirs.

All the practice they'd had at administering their own form of justice through their Clandestine Agency had been in preparation for dealing with Levi. Zeke understood that now, and wouldn't back down from the fight. A small part of his brain still wondered how he could have gotten it so wrong. He reckoned he was a good judge of character and had liked and respected Levi. He had been in the Israeli army for fifteen years, had a spotless record and a wife and two kids whom he supposedly doted on. Of course, he hadn't seen his family since he absconded from captivity, and nor would he ever again. Still, that was not punishment enough for what he'd done to their Cantara. The problem was, they'd spent endless hours and countless resources trying to find the man, without any luck. They had some of the best people in the business at their disposal, but they'd all come up empty-handed. Zeke was starting to think Levi must be dead, which infuriated him because it meant he'd escaped justice, either by taking his own life or being given a helping hand. Unless, until, he and Raoul knew for sure, they would never stop looking for him.

About to go into the bedroom, he paused on the threshold when he heard noises coming from within. Noises he hadn't expected to hear. He didn't need a degree in rocket science to figure out what was going on. A broad smile broke out across his face.

"Well, well," he muttered. "Now that's what I call progress. Hadn't expected her to be up for that quite yet. Leave it to Raoul to change her mind."

But Zeke knew Raoul wouldn't have instigated proceedings. They'd talked about it. Worried over her anxiety if they kissed her too enthusiastically, held her for a little too long, or touched her too intimately. They had learned that any physical contact at all, aside from holding her hand or giving her a chaste kiss, had to come from her. The last thing they wanted to do was spook her, or remind her of aspects of her three-year ordeal she wasn't ready to remember.

He leaned on the door jamb, watching their baby climax. Watching Raoul's ass moving as he gave her what she so obviously needed before taking his own pleasure.

"You guys started without me," he said, strolling into the room with their breakfast and pulling an injured face. "That wasn't nice."

"It was from where I was lying," Cantara replied with a saucy smile.

Zeke laughed, put the tray down, and leaned down to kiss her lips. "I'm real glad about that, babe," he said, tweaking one of her nipples. "You deserved it."

She stretched like the satiated cat she was, her smile wide and smug. "I remembered something," she said, looking excited.

"You did. What was that then?"

"I remembered that you and Raoul both used to play with me like this."

Zeke widened his eyes as a shot a sideways glance Raoul's way. "How do you feel about that, darlin'? Don't tell me you're gonna settle just for this big bad ass," he said, pointing dismissively at Raoul. "I can give you just as much as he can. More in fact."

Raoul flipped him off. "In your dreams, bud."

"Who says anything about choosing?" she asked with a mischievous little smile that moved Zeke's heart. She used to flash that particular smile all the time, but it was the first time he'd seen it since she came home. Progress.

"He is so insecure about his size," Raoul quipped. "Still, I guess he has reason to be."

"You two used to banter like this all the time," Cantara said. "I do remember that much."

"Hey, this isn't banter," Zeke replied, clutching dramatically at his heart. "The size of a man's weapon is no joking matter."

Cantara bit her lip, her eyes coming alight with laughter. "Sorry," she said meekly. "But I didn't start it."

"You okay, darlin'?" Raoul asked. "I didn't hurt you?"

"No, I feel…well, I'm not sure." She sat up and stretched her arms above her head. Zeke was pleased to note there was now enough weight on her tits again for them to bounce when she moved. She had already gained back ten pounds, and all in the right places. "I feel like I'm coming alive."

"Just think how much better you'd be feeling if it was me who'd just fucked you," Zeke said, moving in to steal another kiss.

"You're full of it," Raoul said, unable to stop grinning. "Come on, babe, let's get you cleaned up, then I reckon we could all use some breakfast."

"Poor, Zeke," Cantara said, pouting. "He missed all the fun."

"Oh, don't worry, sweetheart. I've only taken a rain check." He waited until Raoul had returned with a cloth to clean Cantara's pussy with, then moved the breakfast things aside and lay down next to her, pulling her against him. "Tonight, you're mine."

"It's a date."

"Talking of dates, darlin'," Raoul said. "What would you like to do today? More walking?"

"No," Cantara said, sharing a look of determination between them, like she was readying herself for a fight. "I want to ride Iesha."

Zeke glanced at Raoul. "Wadda you think? Is she ready?"

Raoul shrugged. "She was ready to be fucked, so I figure she's strong enough to ride."

"Hey, excuse me, gentlemen, but *she* is in the room."

They laughed aloud. "That's more like it." Zeke swooped in for yet another kiss. "She's getting her sass back. That has to be a good sign."

"Go get yourself showered, darlin'," Raoul said once they'd finished breakfast. "I'll make sure the horses are saddled up for us."

Chapter Ten

"Oh, this is lovely."

Dressed in jeans, a checkered shirt and cowgirl boots, Cantara smiled with delight as she touched the exquisite saddle and bridle Zeke had had handmade for Iesha.

"Not as lovely as it will be to finally see you on her back," Raoul replied, squeezing her waist.

Iesha, recognizing Cantara, whickered a greeting and was rewarded with a carrot. The mare ate her treat and then snuffled around Cantara's pockets, looking for more of the same. Finding none, she arched her neck and gave her head a disgruntled toss, sending her long mane dancing, and pawed irritably at the ground.

"Told you she was precocious," Zeke said. "Iesha, that is, not you, darlin'," he added, blowing Cantara a kiss.

"Sure you're up for this?" Raoul asked.

"Definitely," Cantara replied with firm assurance.

"Okay then, let's get going."

Zeke legged her into the saddle and the guys watched, trying not to show their anxiety, as she gathered up the reins and adjusted her stirrups. They relaxed when Iesha didn't play up, which she sometimes did because she liked to be the center of attention.

"All set?" Raoul asked.

"Will you stop fussing? I'm fine. Besides, if I fall off and take another knock to the head, it might bring my memory back."

Zeke shuddered. "We hadn't thought of that."

"And you are definitely not going to bash your head again," Raoul added, wagging a finger at her.

"Are you guys gonna stand there and stare at us?" she asked, patting Iesha's neck. "Or do you plan on joining us?"

"Baby, you just got yourself an escort," Raoul replied, winking at her as he and Zeke mounted up themselves and rode up on either side of her.

Raoul watched her closely as they rode away from the ranch, worried that this was too much, too soon. He quit fretting when Iesha remembered her manners and Cantara seemed to be as much at home in the saddle as she had been three years previously. Instinct over instruction, he figured, deciding it would be safe to give the horses their heads.

They galloped flat out for several miles. Cantara and Iesha stayed with Raoul and Zeke and their much bigger horses stride for stride. When they finally drew rein, Cantara was laughing. Pure, uninhibited laughter that communicated itself to Zeke and Raoul, who laughed right along with her. This was the way it had always been in Raoul's imagination. Cantara's face was flushed from the exercise, and instead of the wary expression that had disturbed her eyes since her return, they now sparkled with the pure joy of living.

"This mare is a pleasure to ride," Cantara said, patting Iesha's sweaty neck.

"No, darlin'," Raoul replied softly. "The pleasure comes from seeing you shed your inhibitions."

"Isn't that what I did this morning?" she asked, canting her head and sending him a smoldering smile from beneath her tangle of hair.

Zeke laughed. "I'll have to take your word for that." His responding smile was full of wicked intent. "For now."

"It's real pretty out here," Cantara said, taking in the view. "Is this all part of the ranch's land?"

"Yep, as far as the eye can see," Raoul replied.

"I didn't realize I was married to a rich man."

"Aw, darlin', he don't get to take the credit. We only got to buy the land because of my Arapaho blood. They won't sell to anyone without a connection to the tribe."

"He has his uses," Raoul added, grinning.

"Wise guy."

It felt good to be trading insults with Zeke again, Raoul thought. They had stopped their habitual banter once Cantara came home and concentrated on getting her well. Now that she appeared to be on the mend, Raoul could get serious about tracking Levi down. Life couldn't return to normal until they'd exorcised that particular demon.

"I had no idea this lake was here," Cantara said, as she looked out over the expanse of water that had just opened up in front of them. "It's real tranquil out here. Another world."

"You can't see it from the ranch, which is why you didn't know about it," Zeke told her. "In fact, you can't see it from anywhere, unless you do what we've just done and ride out here. There're no roads, no access even by all-terrain vehicles. We have you to ourselves, my dear," he added, waggling his brows at her. "Don't say you haven't been warned."

"Should I fear for my safety?" she asked, fluttering her lashes in mock alarm.

Zeke winked at her. "Absolutely!"

"Come on," Raoul said. "Let's take a break and enjoy the view."

He slid from his saddle and helped Cantara down from hers. Zeke fixed the horses' reins so they couldn't wander too far and left them to graze. The three of them flopped down on the soft grass on the lake's bank, leaning back on their elbows, Cantara in between them, just where they liked her to be. They stared over the wide expanse of water, its surface dappled by sunlight but barely rippled by the soft breeze. The only sound, apart from the horses' bits jangling as they chomped at the grass, was bird song and the occasional buzz on an insect. Peaceful, rural Wyoming at its finest.

Cantara closed her eyes and threw her head back, offering her face up to the sun. "This is paradise," she mumbled.

"Sure is," Raoul agreed. "The best things in life are free, darlin'."

"If you can afford a thousand acre ranch to ensure your privacy," she added, giggling.

"Well, like Zeke said. He does have his uses."

"Hmm, so I hear."

"Witch!" Zeke gently tapped her thigh. "Stop teasing a man who ain't getting any."

"Sorry," she mumbled.

Cantara lay flat on her back, her breathing slowed and it was obvious she'd fallen asleep. Sex followed by the fast ride had sapped her strength, the poor baby. Raoul and Zeke exchanged a smile across her prone body, content to watch her sleep for as long as she needed to. The sun rose higher in the sky, it got a lot hotter and the guys stripped off their shirts.

"What you thinking about?" Zeke asked softly.

"Levi," Raoul replied succinctly. "Where the fuck is he?"

"We need to widen the search. Get more people on it. Don't know about you, but I don't think he's dead."

"Me neither. He had help to break out of jail. The question is, whose help?"

"The Israelis' way of dealing with their own fuck up?"

Raoul shrugged. "I dunno."

"Then what?"

"I think we're missing something. Something obvious."

"We've had three years to worry over it."

"Yeah, but we were feeling so goddamned sorry for ourselves that I still think we weren't firing on all cylinders."

"Yeah, perhaps. Still," Zeke added, nodding toward Cantara. "Now's not the time."

"No, I guess not."

Even so, they continued to discuss the problem in muted tones, their incentive to put their minds to it stretched out between them on the grass, sleeping soundly. Raoul and Zeke were Green Berets—the elite of the elite. No one double-crossed them and lived to tell the tale, and they would have no peace until they figured out what had really happened to almost cost them all their lives. Then it would be retribution time.

* * * *

Cantara loved the feel of the sun on her face, the soft grass beneath her cheek. She felt somnolent after her active morning and closed her eyes, secure in the knowledge that she was safe with Raoul and Zeke to watch over her. She heard them talking across her in quiet voices, but it was too much effort to try and hear what they were saying.

Images of Raoul's flashing eyes, alight with passion and triumph as they made love, reeled through her mind on a continuous loop, heating her up faster than the burning sun could manage. She sensed both guys were keen to fuck her senseless, but was unable to understand why. She winced every time she looked in the mirror. She saw a scrawny body with a gaunt face, sunken eyes, and a haunted expression reflected back at her. Nothing about it was familiar, or attractive. These two hunks could do way better for themselves, but seemed stuck on her.

Who was she to argue?

She rolled over, seeking a more comfortable position, and collided with something rock solid. She sat up with a startled cry, fear flooding her brain.

"Easy, baby, I got you," Zeke said reassuringly.

She felt his strong arms wrap themselves around her in a viselike hold and her panic immediately dissipated. What she'd actually collided with was his chest. A wall of warmth and safety, flowing with rippling muscles—and shirtless. She blinked sleep from her eyes and admired the view.

"It's kinda warm," she mumbled.

"Getting hotter all the time," Zeke replied, looking amused. "You might be better without this."

She briefly panicked when he attacked the buttons on her shirt, popping them free one by one, but just as quickly relaxed. There was no one here to see them and she *was* overheating. He pushed the garment from her shoulders and, like them, she ended up bare-chested.

"Those lovely tits of yours are getting some meat on them again, darlin'," Zeke said, almost sending her into meltdown when his long, capable fingers gently caressed a nipple. "You'll be needing to wear a bra again pretty soon at this rate."

"Hmm."

She closed her eyes and groaned when Zeke attached his lips to the nipple he'd just tweaked.

"You like that, darlin'?" Raoul asked. "You like Zeke sucking your tit?"

"Yes, Master."

"Hey, bud, she remembers how she's supposed to address us." Cantara could hear the satisfaction in Raoul's voice. "That's real good."

Impulsively, Cantara reached out a hand and tugged at the leather thong that Zeke used to tie his hair back. His raven locks cascaded about his shoulders, making him look like a Viking warrior about to ravage her. Well, a girl could hope. Cantara blinked back her surprise when she realized that *was* what she was hoping for. Raoul had fucked her just a few hours ago and now she was ready to take Zeke up on his rain check. Geez! Was that normal?

"Yeah, you used to do that to Zeke all the time," Raoul said from her opposite side, lazily running his fingers down the length of her spine with a gossamer-light touch that made her shiver. "You want Zeke to fuck you right here, out in the open?"

How did he know that? "Yes, please."

The words were out before she could even think if it was what she really wanted. Imagination was one thing. Putting her fantasies into practice was entirely another. Zeke lifted his lips from her breast and transferred them to her lips, engulfing her in a drugging kiss that blew her mind and swept away her lingering doubts. Raoul's fingers had slipped between the waistband at the back of her jeans, which were too big for her, and were playing with the tops of her buttocks. She instinctively shoved her backside up harder against those fingers, hazy recollections in her confused mind telling her she used to enjoy what he was trying to do to her. She felt another hand—Zeke's presumably—unsnapping her jeans and jerking down the zip. She was too engrossed in kissing Zeke back to pay much notice.

A little squeal of protest slipped out when Raoul abandoned her butt. Zeke increased the pressure of his arms, and his lips, and it didn't seem to matter anymore. But Raoul obviously wasn't done with her, because she felt one of her boots being pulled from her foot. Then the other. Then her socks. Raoul picked up one foot and gently sucked her toes, one at a time, his tongue tantalizing and teasing like only he knew how to. Sizzling sensations worked their way up her legs, homing in on her leaking pussy. Finding it impossible to sit still, Cantara wriggled about in Zeke's arms.

"I think the lady needs fucking," Zeke said huskily, breaking the kiss, sounding like he was in urgent need, too.

"Then get to it, partner."

Zeke lifted her and Raoul pulled her jeans smoothly away, leaving her in the open air wearing nothing more protective than a skimpy pair of panties.

"Hmm," Zeke said, his eyes shimmering with hot intentions as he held her at arm's length and looked his fill. "Ain't that just about the prettiest sight you ever did see?"

"No arguments this end," Raoul agreed, lowering his head and planting a kiss on one of her buttocks.

Zeke released her, stood up, and shed his boots and jeans. He was rock hard, his pulsating cock jutting aggressively from the juncture of tapering hips and strong thighs.

"Get on your hands and knees for me, darlin'," he said, a rough edge to his voice. "We need to play a bit more before we get it on."

Cantara scurried into position, feeling as though she had done this before. A lot of times. It was so frustrating that she couldn't remember when, but knew it must have been with the two of them. The cloying mist inside her head that shrouded her past cleared more frequently now, but never for long enough for her to be able to hold on to the memories that filtered through it. The guys said it didn't matter, they could tell her whatever she needed to know. But they couldn't. They had no idea what had happened to her during the three years she had been held captive by a man who was supposedly related to her by marriage, but of whom she had no recollection whatsoever.

Her mind was brought back to the here and now when she felt Zeke kneeling behind her. Her pulse quickened when he pulled her panties down and started to play with her pussy. She was embarrassed when she felt her juices trickling down the insides of her thighs, but Zeke laughed and seemed pleased that she'd started without him. He nudged her legs wider apart and lapped up the spill with the tip of his tongue. It was the most exquisite torture, especially when his lips latched onto her clit and sucked her entire nub into her mouth. She screamed and bucked her pelvis deeper into his mouth.

"Seems she likes what you're doing to her, bud," Raoul said, sounding amused. "But then she always did have the most sensitive clit in the universe."

Cantara felt her entire body tremble when Raoul's handsome face appeared sideways beneath her and he applied his tongue to her breasts. He used his fingers, too, sending spikes of lust dancing through her nervous system. She cried out when he bit down on a nipple, and then sucked it hard. Pain and pleasure chased one another through her bloodstream, intermingling until they were indistinguishable. She liked pain. The flash of memory was presumably ignited by the bite, because Cantara knew it was true. She instinctively controlled her breathing and the next time Raoul did an experimental bite she was ready to absorb the pain and allow it easier access to her pleasure phonemes.

Zeke rubbed his rigid cock between the crack in her butt while Raoul continued to work on her tits. She sensed some sort of message pass between them, after which Zeke brought his hand down lightly over her buttocks. She gasped, but again absorbed the tingling, every cell in her body aroused by it. Her heart kicked up another notch when, working in seamless tandem, Raoul bit lightly at her solidified nipples while Zeke lightly paddled her butt. It was the most exquisite torture. Cantara threw her head back and roared, feeling wanton, desirable and, most importantly of all, truly alive again.

"I'd sure like to fuck your ass, darlin'," Zeke muttered in her ear. "Just the way you used to like it. You loved having one of our big cocks filling your backside. You couldn't get enough of it. Problem is, I didn't plan to do this to you out here. Course, you only have yourself to blame for that. You're so fucking sexy that I walk around with a permanent hard-on. Still, I don't have any lube and don't wanna hurt you, so I guess I'm just gonna have to make the most of that hot little pussy of yours. Would you like that?"

"Yes! God, yes!"

Zeke chuckled. "Just checkin'."

She felt his fingers part her folds and half expected him to delve inside with several digits. Instead she felt the head of his massive erection nudging against her entrance and pushed back to welcome him inside. The connection was made with smooth fluidity and he set up a hot, slick tempo as he filled her to capacity with his throbbing need.

"You okay, darlin'?" he asked, grabbing her hips and guiding himself deeper inside.

"Yes, it feels like heaven."

"You got that part right."

Raoul was now tugging at one of her nipples with his teeth, pulling it so far from her body that she thought he might tug it clean off. But he knew what he was doing. Just at the last possible moment, he released it, sending liquid desire rushing through her with the restoration of the blood flow. Helpless against the raging force of her need, she moved in sync with Zeke, aware of her orgasm building fast as tingling exhilaration afflicted her limbs, her psyche, every damned inch of her. The physical alchemy that existed between her and these two Greek gods whipped her into a vortex of need and she surrendered herself completely to their very capable hands.

Something was nagging at the back of her addled brain. Something about not climaxing without permission. No way! On sensory overload, passions stirred to the point of madness, there wasn't a thing in the world she could have done to stop the onslaught, even if she'd wanted to, which she most emphatically did not. She had earned the right to have some fun.

"Zeke, fuck me harder!"

"You got it, darlin'."

He slammed into her, his loaded balls slapping against her buttocks as he gave her what she so badly need. Passion tugged at her on a level over which she had no control when Raoul nipped harder than ever at her nipple. It was too much to endure. She clamped her sheath tight around Zeke's cock, holding him captive deep inside her, and exploded.

"Yes!" She threw her head back and howled the word. "That's what I need. Don't stop, Zeke. I'm still coming."

"You and me both, sweetheart."

He grunted and slammed into her once, and then again. She felt his cock spasm and sperm shoot into her in an endless stream, his body a hot prison over hers, slick with dewy sweat as he continued to work her cunt. Her orgasm reignited and she moved with him until, finally, just when she thought the pleasure would be too much to endure, her body stopped pulsating.

Cantara rolled onto her back and threw an arm over each of her men's abdomens, laughing and crying tears of joy at the same time.

"Welcome back," Raoul said, leaning over to place a chaste kiss on her lips.

* * * *

"There's only one way to get clean out here, darlin'." Raoul smiled at Cantara, loving the way she radiated beauty with that *just-fucked* look in her eye. Then he transferred his glance to the glistening surface of the lake. "Fancy skinny-dipping?"

He stood up and shed his jeans. He was painfully erect, but turned his back to her so she wouldn't see. The cold water would deal with his woody. No reason for her to feel pressured. She'd already done way more than Raoul would have expected of her today, embracing their needs and her own with unbridled enthusiasm. He heard Zeke and Cantara scrambling to their feet and watched them run hand in hand to the water's edge, giggling like kids. Cantara shrieked when the water lapped against her toes.

"It's freezing! I'm not getting in there."

"It's only cold because you're so hot," Zeke told her.

Hot in every damned way.

"Easy for you to say." She turned and beckoned to Raoul. "Come on, big guy. This was your idea. No wimping out on us."

Raoul ran to the bank and dove straight under the water. The cold water had the desired effect and his hard-on withered. What a waste! He surfaced, pushed the wet hair away from his eyes and trod water as he waved them on in.

"Did someone say something about being a wimp?" he asked. "Under normal circumstances, that would be the sort of talk to get a person spanked."

"Did I say something wrong?" Cantara asked with faux innocence and an exaggerated flutter of her lashes.

Zeke laughed and took the plunge, surfacing next to Raoul. "Come on, babe," he said. "You'll be glad you did."

Cantara shrugged, took a deep breath and pushed elegantly into the water. She dipped her head beneath it, and then surfaced again, spluttering and laughing. "Race you to the other bank," she said, setting off before they realized what she had planned.

Of course they could have beaten her easily, but they let her win, if only for the pleasure they got from following close behind her cute butt and admiring the way it cut through the water. She was breathless and laughing when she reached the other side.

"You're right," she said, rolling onto her back and floating, staring up at the cloudless sky. "It's invigorating."

Raoul couldn't resist. He dove beneath her, came up right under her, and scooped her into his arms.

"Glad to see you having fun, darlin'," he said, kissing her wet lips.

"I am, thanks to you guys."

"That's real good, but there's just one problem I've got."

"Not again," she said, with a martyred sigh.

"Oh, that's always a problem when I'm anywhere near you," Raoul replied, feeling his cock stirring again, even in the cold water, simply because he was holding her in his arms. "But this is way more serious."

She flexed her brows. "More serious than sex? I know my memory's not all it could be, but I seem to recall that nothing was more serious for you guys than getting it on."

"Ah, but darlin', you insulted my manhood. That wasn't nice."

"I did?" She opened her eyes very wide—all wet lashes and feigned innocence. "What did I do?"

Zeke's amused chuckle rang out. "She didn't find anything to insult about mine."

"Did you have something to say about someone being a wuss?" Raoul asked, ignoring Zeke's banter.

Before she could answer, he tossed her in the air and let her fall back into the water. She squealed with laughter, swam over to Zeke, and whispered protractedly in his ear. Her eyes danced as she glanced back at Raoul. With a squeal of laughter she swam over to him and splashed him from behind. Before he could retaliate, she set off for the other bank, as sleek and graceful through the water as an otter. Raoul matched her stroke for stroke, sending her an egregious grin as he plotted his next move.

"We all make our own choices in this world, sweetheart," he said, wagging a finger at her when their feet hit the shallows on the side of the lake. The horses looked up to see what the commotion was about, then went back to their grazing.

Cantara was in an uninhibited mood, out to have fun. He expected a pithy retort but instead she stood stock still in the shallow water and gaped at him.

"What is it, babe?" Raoul rushed to her side, sensing a swift swing in her mood that bothered him.

"What did you just say?" she asked. Her eyes had lost their sparkle, and the haunted expression he'd hoped never to see again returned to her features.

"We all make our own choices." Raoul shared a look with Zeke and shrugged, unable to figure out what had gotten to her. "It was just an off the cuff remark. I didn't mean anything by it. I sure didn't mean to upset you."

"But you didn't, you made me remember."

"My comment made you remember." Raoul was totally bewildered. "Made you remember what?"

"All of it." She sucked in a shuddering breath, trembling from head to foot. "It was what Salim kept saying to me. The fog's gone. I remember everything that happened to me after I was captured."

Chapter Eleven

A thousand dire recollections of her three-year ordeal chased one another through Cantara's mind. Her head throbbed and her limbs trembled as she was swept back in her imagination to the dank prison that she had thought would become her tomb. She had spent the past month living in a bubble, unsure of her history, her identity—unsure of anything except the unshakable certainty that she was supposed to be with Raoul and Zeke. Now that she remembered the cold hard reality of how she'd gotten a second chance to be with them, she belatedly realized that ignorance had been bliss.

"Come on, darlin'," Raoul said, sweeping her into his arms and carrying her out of the lake. "Let's get you warm and dry. You're shaking like a goddamned leaf."

Zeke produced a towel from his saddlebags and rubbed Cantara's limbs briskly with it. "Let's get your circulation going again, sweet thing," he said. "Then you can tell us what you remember. It might help to talk about it."

When her body was dry, Raoul helped her back into her clothing and Zeke set about towel-drying her hair. She was incapable of helping herself and stood compliantly where she was while they took care of her. The initial shock of recollection was wearing off and, at first reluctant to speak of the horrors she had endured, she now wanted to share them with the only two people in the world who could possibly understand.

The two men whom she loved unconditionally. The only family she now had. The only family she would ever need.

"Better?" Raoul asked, gently kissing her brow as he took her hand, sat down on the grass, and pulled her down with him.

"Yes, I think so."

"That's good." Raoul's reassuring smile helped her to emerge from the pain of recollection. "You remember your family now."

It wasn't a question, and Cantara merely nodded. "It feels like I'm grieving for them all over again," she said, wiping away an errant tear.

"I imagine it must," Zeke said, stroking her arm. "But the special thing about you is that you didn't want revenge, like the majority of people in your situation would have."

"Like my brothers did?"

"Right. You could see the futility of violence, wanted to try and put a stop to it. You were absolutely determined to make a difference. That takes real courage, especially when so many people tried to dissuade you." Zeke paused. "Us included."

"I should have listened." She looked from one to the other of them, tears streaming down her face. "I thought you were dead," she said bleakly. "Which meant my life was over, too, because I couldn't imagine living without you, even if I could get past the guilt."

"Oh, darlin'!" Raoul pulled her into his arms and she found sanctuary against the solidity of his granite chest. "We thought the same thing about you." He nuzzled the top of her wet head with his lips. "Do you imagine we would have stopped looking for you if we thought there was even an outside chance you were still alive?"

"No, I'm sure you wouldn't have, so I guess that means I'm glad you thought I was dead. You never would have found me, and would probably have gotten yourselves killed in the hunt. You know how volatile things are on the West Bank."

"We know," Zeke said. "But it wouldn't have stopped us."

Cantara didn't quite know how she finished up there, but she was now sitting on Raoul's lap. He and Zeke were still naked, which didn't appear to bother them, and Zeke pulled her legs over his groin, so they each had a part of her to touch with their skilled fingers, to comfort, to caress. Now that they had taken control over her body, showing her through their fierce desire to protect her just how much she was loved, Cantara's mind felt better able to face her memories. They were just memories. They couldn't hurt her now.

"What happened to you?" she asked.

"We followed you, as agreed, but sensed from the get-go that something wasn't right," Raoul replied. "But it was too late to turn back because we had no way of pulling you out. That was stupid. We should have insisted on a failsafe of some sort. Anyway, they had you and we weren't about to let you out of our sight."

"But we rode that damned motorbike straight into an ambush," Zeke said. "They knew we'd be following you, knew what we were to you, and planned to take us out. We couldn't figure out why at the time. Now we know it was personal because Salim wanted you for himself, it makes more sense."

"I'm so very sorry," she said, shaking her head against Raoul's chest.

"It's not your fault, darlin'," Raoul said. "We were taken, held for a week, but we managed to break out. We dealt with the guards and the head honcho guarding us and managed to get back to base. But we only escaped after we'd been shown a video of you…" Raoul choked on the words and took a moment to compose himself. It was Cantara's turn to comfort him by gently caressing his face with the tips of her fingers, running one of them across his lips until he expelled a soft sigh and continued talking. "You were tied to a chair. A man approached you. He had his back to the camera so we never were able to identify him. Anyway, he slapped you so hard that you fell to the ground."

"Which must be how you fractured your skull," Zeke added. "There was so much blood. It killed us to see it, but we couldn't show any reaction to that damned psychopath who was holding us. We were denying all personal connections to you, you see, but he didn't believe us. Then we saw you laid out, eyes dead and staring, on a bed. It damned near did our captors' work for them and finished us off then and there."

"They tortured you," she said on a whisper, fresh tears flowing. "All because of me. I can't stand it."

"We're big boys, darlin'," Zeke assured her. "We got through it, and got our revenge, at least on the guys who held us."

"That was after they showed us the video of your dead body," Raoul explained, his Adam's apple bobbing as he swallowed down his emotion. "We couldn't risk escaping all the time we thought you were still alive, or they would have taken it out on you. Once they showed us that fucking video, the effect of which I'll never forget, we figured there was nothing left for us to lose." He ran his hand possessively down the curve of her face. "We had lost our reason for living because we were stupid enough to fall for their cheap trick. Our training was better than that. We never should have believed second-hand evidence like that."

"One damned thing that idiot Pool was right about was our being too close to you to be objective," Zeke explained. "Anyone else and we would most likely have seen through the ruse."

"They did something similar with me." Cantara froze at the memory.

"What did they do, honey?" Zeke asked.

"They showed me a picture of the two of you, naked, bloodied and apparently dead." A series of shudders shook her body. "I died with you that day because I had nothing left to live for."

"Probably taken in the cell where they kept us while we were asleep," Raoul replied.

"Tell us what happened to you, from the beginning," Zeke said.

"Unlike you, I didn't realize things weren't going according to plan. Until...well, until they took me, not to meet with the separatists, but to a private house. I was taken into a small room, given some tea, and told to wait." Cantara stared at the lake without seeing it, reliving her version of hell. "I started to get anxious when I was kept waiting for too long, *and* when I realized I'd been locked in. Then, eventually, Salim came into the room, which is when I knew I'd been duped and I wasn't there to broker peace. You were right to say they'd never let a woman get involved." She shook her head. "Salim always gave me the creeps. He played the role of the bookish researcher, always in his brother's shadow—"

"His brother being your husband, Jordan," Zeke clarified.

"Right. Jordan was the accredited academic. No one thought Salim was his intellectual equal because he never gave them any reason to think that way. He crept about like a wraith, always seeming to turn up wherever I happened to be, as though he was spying on me. I was polite, but tried never to be alone with him. It was the way he looked at me that really freaked me out. But when I mentioned it to Jordan he just laughed and said I was imagining things. Salim was his brother. It was only natural that he would watch over me when Jordan wasn't around, and that he only wanted to protect me."

"I'm guessing Salim was the leader of the separatist group you were trying to talk to," Zeke said.

"Right." Cantara replied, scowling. "And he was the one who encouraged my brothers to join them, then sent them on a suicide mission. He was very proud of that fact and told me good, loyal Palestinians had a duty to stand up for their country."

"And die for it," Raoul muttered through clenched teeth.

"He seemed to think I would be grateful," Cantara explained, puffing out her cheeks indignantly.

"He went to considerable trouble to get you alone," Zeke said. "I'm almost afraid to ask what he wanted."

"What he wanted was me," she replied, shuddering. "He said he had always known we were supposed to be together and didn't blame me for trying to interfere in men's business. He said grief must have warped my mind and he had a duty to look after me. It was what Jordan would have wanted him to do."

"Oh, baby!" Raoul held her a little tighter. "The man sounds as though he was deluded."

"And dangerous," Zeke added, massaging the instep of her left foot, his expression thunderous.

"I told him I'd made a mistake and needed to leave, which was when his personality underwent a complete change. He was no longer the meek, eager to please little man I remembered. He turned into a maniac, throwing things around the room, ranting about my head having been turned by the Americans and Israelis and not knowing who I was anymore. I was scared, I'll admit that much—"

"Of course you were," Raoul said soothingly.

"Then it was like someone turned a switch and he was calm again. He offered me food, which I refused, and that angered him. He locked me in the cellar then and I must have been there…well, certainly overnight, and it was some time into the next day before he opened the door."

"Did you see anyone else?" Zeke asked.

"Not at that time, but people came and went later on."

"Did you recognize any of them?" Raoul asked. "Pool and Hassan will be interested, but we can think about that later. Go on with your story, darlin'."

"He came in the next day and asked if I had come to my senses. I basically told him to get lost, which is when he hit me for the first time." She shook her head. "I was clinging to the hope that you guys would be on my tail, and that rescue was at hand. I can't tell you how desperate I felt when he took great pleasure in telling me you were both dead. I knew I wasn't supposed to react to the mention of your name, Raoul, but I guess I'm not a very good actress. He actually laughed, the bastard enjoyed my despondency, and told me I would always be let down if I put my faith in Americans."

"He sounds like a real piece of work," Zeke said.

"I told him I had no idea what he was talking about, which is when he showed me the video of the two of you, looking beaten and dead. I lost it then and fell apart." Cantara impatiently swiped away fresh tears. "I had nothing left to live for, but was damned if I'd give myself to Salim, just to try and find an opportunity to escape. I had nothing left to escape to without you guys," she added softly. "When he tried to comfort me I used some of the self-defense techniques you'd taught me and landed him on his ass. I think I hurt him pretty bad. His body and his pride."

"Good!" both guys said together.

"He was like an enraged bull after that. He tried again and I kicked him in the balls so hard that I think I might have ruptured one of them. He howled with pain, and threatened me with all sorts of dire consequences. I told him I'd rather be dead than have him touch me, and if he tried to come near me again he'd get more of the same. I was almost as tall as him and a damned sight fitter, so I think I scared him. Anyway, he called two other men in. I fought them like mad but they were too strong for me. They tied me to that chair and Salim hit me hard enough to knock me off it, which must be when I fractured my skull. I now remember waking up in that cellar with my head bandaged and a throbbing pain inside of it."

"Poor baby," Raoul soothed. "It's a damned shame the slime ball is dead. He's robbed me of the pleasure of detaching his head from his frigging body. Slowly and painfully."

"He came in to see me, all smiles again, and said I only had myself to blame for what he'd been forced to do to me."

"Scum like that always find a way to blame others for their own actions," Zeke said, scowling.

"Don't I know it." Cantara convulsed at the revisited memory. "He kept me in the cellar all the time after that, and told me no one would ever find me. I believed him. But he also didn't try to touch me again."

"Thank fuck for that," both guys said together.

"I think he must have seen something in me that told him I was serious. Even in my weakened condition, I could still probably have taken him and he knew it. So, he came down every day, offering me decent food instead of the swill I was given the rest of the time, if I would do one small thing for him in return. Touch his hand, smile at him, innocuous things like that. The smell of the food was tempting, but I kept thinking he'd had you two killed, and was damned if I'd give an inch. It infuriated him, which is when he would take a whip to me, or amuse himself by nicking my skin with a knife, stuff like that. Other times he just sat looking at me for hours on end, rubbing his cock, bringing himself off."

Raoul and Zeke scowled, obviously remembering the state of her body when she'd been rescued. Some of the scars would never disappear completely.

"I didn't care about the psychological torture, just so long as he didn't try it on again, which he never did. He just kept trying to wear me down with the carrot and stick approach, telling me I'd thank him in the end for reminding me where my loyalties ought to be. I was a Palestinian woman with a duty to have sons."

"With him, I suppose," Zeke said, scowling.

"Yeah."

"And that went on for three years," Raoul said, shaking his head. "He was a damned patient man."

"Oh yes, stubborn was his middle name. Think about it, Raoul, he spent all those years playing second fiddle to his peace-loving brother, pretending he was of the same persuasion. But all the time he was heading up one of the most extreme factions in the PLO and no one close to him even suspected. He was a man who always got his own way, no matter how long he had to wait to make it happen."

"They'll never be peace in the region with men like him on the loose," Zeke said, sounding resigned.

"You were right to tell me not to go," Cantara said, sharing a glance between them. "I'm sorry I was so stubborn. It was arrogant of me to think I could make a difference. I should have listened to you."

"You did what you had to do, babe," Raoul replied, kissing her. "We both admire the heck out of you for that."

"What I don't understand is who told Salim you and I were married, Raoul? It was kept secret for precisely the reason that the Palestinians might not like it."

"Levi was the guilty party," Zeke said.

"What, Colonel Hassan's adjutant?" She frowned. "I don't believe it. He seemed like such a regular guy."

"Well, that just goes to show you never can tell," Raoul replied. "They found stuff buried on his personal computer. E-mails between him and a woman. He'd been set up and had no choice but to pass on intel or he would lose his job, his liberty, and his family."

"He loved his family. I can't see him cheating on his wife or doing anything to risk his kids' safety," Cantara said, shaking her head. "I remember him showing me a picture of his wife and kids once and telling me how much he admired what I was trying to do. He wanted peace in the region, too, for his family's sake. He was a liberal-minded Israeli who accepted there was room for both sides to live in peace, if there was the will."

"Yeah, we thought that way about him, too," Zeke said. "But it wasn't our call. We were prepared to tear anyone apart in revenge for your death on the flimsiest of evidence, so we didn't ask too many questions at the time."

"Where is he now?" Cantara asked. "In an Israeli prison, presumably, but we ought to go and talk to him, find out—"

"He escaped from custody," Raoul told her.

"What! You're kidding me. No one escapes from the Israelis." She paused. "Unless they want them to."

"We've been looking for him ever since he absconded," Zeke said. "And we have some pretty good means at our disposal, thanks to the Agency."

"Is that why you started it?" she asked.

"I guess," Raoul said. "We'd had it with the army after we thought you were dead. We were fed up with obeying stupid orders, playing by the rules when the scumbags got away with just about anything and everything. We decided to level the playing field and now we get a ton of work from the military, who don't want to be seen to wash their dirty linen in public," Raoul expelled a mirthless chuckle. "How's that for irony?"

"I'm gonna play devil's advocate here," Cantara said. "Let's say, for the sake of argument, that it wasn't Levi who spilled the beans. Who else knew we were married, Raoul?"

"Pool," Raoul and Zeke said together.

"I never liked the jerk," Raoul added alone, "and wouldn't put anything past him."

"He was very anxious to talk to Cantara at Andrews," Zeke said. "And since he's now riding a desk, I don't see why he needed to. Unless he was worried that she might have heard his name mentioned while in captivity."

"We need to take a closer look at him," Raoul agreed. "Should have done it before now."

"Yeah, well." Zeke stretched his arms above his head. "Hindsight's a damned irritating bastard."

"They keep ringing, Pool and Parker, to see if they can come and talk to you, Cantara," Raoul explained. "But I think we'll hold them off for a while longer yet, until we've done more digging of our own and know who to trust."

"Whatever you think best," she replied. "I'm in no hurry to talk to them."

"The only other person who could possibly have known about the marriage was Pool's adjutant, Romney," Raoul said. "It's not in writing anywhere but adjutants know everything, even the things they aren't officially supposed to know. It's the only way they can perform efficiently."

"Someone else to look at, then," Zeke said. "Or, we could just let it go. We've got Cantara back and that's all that really matters."

"No." Cantara and Raoul spoke together.

"No," she repeated alone. "I lost three years of my life and I need to know who to blame for that. And, knowing you two as well as I do, I suspect neither of you will be completely comfortable unless you get some answers, too. Why else would you turn yourselves into vigilantes-cum-detectives?"

"Gotta hand it to our gal," Zeke said, swooping in for a kiss. "She knows us pretty damned well."

"It's been eating away at us," Raoul agreed. "So yeah, if you don't think it will set your recovery back, let's do some in depth digging."

"How do you feel, darlin'?" Zeke asked. "Now that you remember it all."

"Better," Cantara said, because it was true. The shock, the disgust, even the guilt at what she had led the guys into, had worn off quicker than it should have done. "Talking to you about it, knowing you understand and forgive me, has saved you the cost of a shrink."

Raoul and Zeke shot her identically surprised looks. "We didn't say anything about you needing a shrink."

"I heard you talking about it one night when I couldn't sleep. In your position, I would have been thinking about engaging one as well, but I'm glad you don't have to. I'd much rather bare everything to you guys. In all respects." She leaned up to gently kiss Raoul's lips, then leaned forward so she could repeat the process with Zeke. "Thank you for being so patient with me."

"Darlin', nothing's too much trouble for you." Raoul ran the fingers of one hand across her nape. "We love you. Don't you get that part yet?"

"We're nothing without you, babe," Zeke added, resuming her foot massage. "And as for Washington here, he's been like a bear with a three-year sore head."

"Oh, and you've been all peace and goodwill?"

"Stop it, you two." Cantara laughed at their banter. "Don't make me pick sides."

"That we would never do," Raoul replied, his grin fading. "In case you've forgotten, and if you have we'd be happy to remind you, that we like to share you." His eyes smoldered with wicked intent as he raked her body with a slow, sexy gaze. "We like it a lot."

Cantara moistened her lips, wondering how they could have gotten so dry without her realizing it. "I have vague recollections," she mused. "But what with my memory still being so spotty, I guess it wouldn't hurt to go on a refresher course."

Zeke roared with laughter. "We've got our baby back, bud, no question."

"So it seems." Raoul expelled an exaggerated sigh. "Looks like we're gonna have our work cut out keeping her in line. No way is she ready to play rough with us again yet. She needs to get her strength back first."

"Does *she* get to have any say in the matter?"

"No," Raoul and Zeke replied together.

Cantara pouted. "Spoil sports!"

"We ought to get back and start thinking about how we're gonna nail Levi, or whoever it was who gave away our secret," Raoul said, chuckling at her disgruntled expression.

They stood up, and Cantara was treated to full frontal views of her naked decadent gods. All taut flesh over hard muscle, plenty of natural definition, plenty more raw animal vitality that made her salivate with anticipation. Despite what Raoul might think, she knew she wouldn't have much trouble getting them to resume normal activities of a sexual nature, and that was precisely what she planned to do when they got back to the ranch. Now that she had her memory back, she needed to take control of her life again. If she behaved like a damaged wilting violet then Salim would have won, which was not an option. She needed to be in charge of her own destiny and appreciate this second chance she'd been given.

"Planning to ride home like that, boys?" she asked, cutting them a wicked grin.

Raoul swatted her backside as he pulled on his jeans. "Glad to see you feeling so much better, hon," he said, blowing her a kiss.

Once they were dressed, Zeke rounded up the horses and this time she mounted up without needing their help. As they cantered back to the ranch side by side, Cantara reveled in the feel of the wind blowing through her hair, of the simple joy of life, of the even greater joy of having Raoul and Zeke all to herself. She glanced from one of them to the other, aware from their grim expressions that they had vengeance on their minds.

Cantara, on the other hand, had sex games on hers.

Chapter Twelve

Raoul looked up from his laptop and frowned. "Cantara's been gone a long time. You think she's all right?"

They had finished dinner and she'd excused herself for a moment. Wrapped up in reading the latest findings on Levi, supplied thanks to some creative hacking on the part of Mark and Karl, Raoul hadn't noticed the time passing.

"I'll go check on her."

Zeke left his own computer and sauntered down to the yellow room. "Hey, babe, you okay?" He paused and Raoul heard his sharp intake of breath. "Holy shit! Raoul, get down here. You need to see this."

In a panic, thinking she'd had a bad reaction to her awakened memories, Raoul flew down the corridor in record time. She had been too calm, too casual, about what she had remembered. Raoul, unsurprised by her a delayed reaction, was ready to comfort and console. When he saw what actually awaited him, he screeched to a halt immediately behind Zeke.

"Fucking hell!"

"Hey, guys, what kept you?"

Cantara lay on the bed wearing a black corset trimmed with scarlet lace, held together at the front by a crisscrossed ribbon. Raoul remembered buying it for her just before they left the States for Israel. She hadn't gotten around to wearing it—until now. It was pulled so tight that Raoul figured he could have spanned her waist with his two hands. Her tits looked disproportionately large and spilled out of the top of the garment. He could see the edges of her raspberry-pink areolas and the outline of her nipples through the satin material. She wore sheer stockings held up by suspenders, leaving a good six inches of bare upper thigh to be kissed and caressed. Her feet were encased in shoes with four-inch spiky heels. Her knees were bent up, her legs spread to give them an up-close view of her freshly shaved pussy. But the most extraordinary part of it all was that she had found their handcuffs and attached one wrist to the headboard.

"I couldn't fix the other one myself," she said, pouting. "I need your help for that." She giggled. "Well, that and a few other things."

"Er, what do you think you're doing?" Raoul asked, even though it was pretty damned obvious. His cock was standing to attention and taking an active interest in proceedings.

"Don't you wanna play?" she asked with a sultry smile that said she knew damned well they did.

"Do we ever," Zeke muttered. "But you're not strong enough for this yet."

"Says who?"

"Fuck it!" Raoul breathed.

"That's kinda the idea," Cantara replied, her unfettered hand drifting to play with her pussy, from which her juices were freely flowing.

Raoul and Zeke exchanged a loaded glance. How the fuck were they supposed to resist her when she put on such a provocative display? Raoul's cock pulsated painfully inside his jeans. If he unzipped and gave it the breathing room it needed, he would be lost. Part of him was delirious with joy because Cantara wanted to rough and tumble with them again so soon after her ordeal. The problem was, he and Zeke liked to play hard, and seriously. Pain was an integral part of their pleasure, and Cantara had had way too much pain over the past three years for them to knowingly inflict more.

"Stop overthinking it, big guy." Cantara addressed her remark to Raoul. "I remember everything you used to do to me. The spankings, the punishments, both of you fucking me at once." Her eyes sparkled with a combination of desire and determination. She wouldn't be easily dissuaded. Whether Raoul actually wanted to dissuade her was open to debate. "I want all that again, and I won't have you holding back out of some misguided sense of responsibility. I know what I'm asking of you, but you need to understand that it's real important to me to feel I'm living life to the full again."

"I guess we can play, bud," Zeke said. "Doesn't mean we have to take her too far."

"Oh no!" Cantara aimed a cool gaze at Zeke. "I want it all. Don't you dare think about short-changing me. You said it yourselves, I've been through a lot. We all have, and we deserve to have some fun. We've been given a second chance. Let's not blow it."

Raoul shrugged, through with trying to talk himself out of something all three of them wanted pretty damned desperately. "Okay, darlin', if you're absolutely sure."

"Is there something about this outfit that makes you think I'm not?"

Raoul laughed. "I hear you, but first off you need to be punished."

"At last, they get it," she replied, rolling her eyes, probably aware that sarcasm would definitely earn her a spanking.

Raoul and Zeke unzipped in unison. Two large erections sprang free from their flies, jutting halfway up their bellies. Cantara glanced at them, widened her eyes in evident appreciation and then giggled.

"Doesn't look as though you needed too much persuading after all."

"What do we remember about speaking only when spoken to?" Raoul asked, wagging a finger at her.

Cantara immediately lowered her eyes and lay passively on the bed, legs demurely closed together. "Sorry, Masters."

"That's better," Zeke said, reaching over to release the handcuffs.

Raoul rummaged in the cupboard that housed all the toys they'd never thought they would get to use on Cantara. The cupboard where she'd found the handcuffs. She wanted to be spanked and Raoul was willing to oblige, but they needed to take this gently. Hurt her without hurting her. Bring her to life slowly, explore her limits, her desires, her demands. Never had the responsibility of being Doms hung more heavily on their shoulders. Never had it mattered more that they…well, strike the right balance.

"Go and crouch in the corner with your back to the room while we decide upon your punishment, Cantara."

"Yes, Masters."

They both watched the sway of her hips as she sauntered across the room in her tarty shoes and slowly crouched down, deliberately sticking her bare ass in the air, the provocative little witch!

"She won't settle for just your hand, bud," Zeke said, shaking his head in admiration. "She's up for the complete deal already. It's our duty not to disappoint her."

"But we have a duty of care, also. She's been through so much. Can she actually take what she's asking us to dish out?"

"She's so damned turned on, I reckon she can take a spanking. Don't reckon we can both fuck her at the same time quite yet, though."

"Me neither, but there is another way."

Raoul voiced his suggestion. Zeke grinned and nodded.

"Works for me," he said.

"I figured it might." Raoul picked up a horsehair warm-up flogger, the gentlest piece of equipment he owned, and tried it across his hand. It caused a pleasant sting. "That'll do it," he said, nodding his approval.

Raoul sat on the edge of the bed with the flogger, while Zeke leaned against the wall, arms folded, ready to watch the show.

"Come here, Cantara," Raoul said in his deep Dom's voice.

She elegantly rose to her feet, turned slowly and walked across to him, eyes downcast, but not so low that Raoul didn't catch the glint of anticipation in them. Their little sub was turned on, big time. Still fully clothed, with only his cock hanging out, Raoul indicated the floor in front of him and Cantara dutifully knelt in front of him.

"Do you have something to say to me?" he asked her.

"Yes, Sir. I've been real bad."

"What did you do that was so bad?"

"I asked you and Master Zeke to fuck me."

"And why is that wrong?"

"I'm not allowed to say what I want. It's my job to please you, not the other way around."

"So it is." Raoul shared a look with Zeke, glad she remembered her training. "So, what should we do about it?"

"I need to be punished, Master. Please punish me. Beat the badness out of me."

"I guess you do need to be taught a lesson. Get up and lay across my knees."

When she had done so, Raoul rested the flogger against her buttocks. "Remember to control your breathing, darlin'. Safe word me if it gets too much."

Raoul brought the flogger down gently.

"I can't feel it," she complained from beneath the curtain of hair covering her face.

Raoul shrugged at Zeke, who shrugged right back. It was apparent Cantara was in no mood to settle for half measures, so Raoul repeated the process with a little more vigor. His efforts were rewarded with a sharp intake of breath from Cantara, then a sigh of contentment. Raoul continued to punish her, at the same time reaching beneath her with the fingers of his other hand and applying them to her swollen clit. She squirmed on his knee, clearly loving what he was doing to her. Raoul's heart soared at the sight of her cute butt, striped pink from the flogger, and from the enthusiasm of her response.

When Raoul figured she'd taken enough, he threw the flogger aside and told her to get up. She stood before him in her sexy corset, eyes downcast, biting her lip to suppress a rogue smile.

"Do you have something to say to me, Cantara?"

"Yes, Master. Thank you for chastising me. I deserved it."

"Yeah, you did. Now get back on the bed, on your hands and knees."

"Yes, Sir."

Both men paused to admire a view that a few shorts weeks ago they'd only thought ever to see again in their imaginations, then stripped off their clothes. Zeke slid sideways beneath Cantara and applied his attention to her tits, poking provocatively out of the corset. He helped them the rest of the way out and attached his lips to a solidified nipple. Raoul claimed her ass for his own and ran a finger, slick with lube, down her crack. She flinched, but quickly settled again, distracted by Zeke's gentle torture.

"You remember when we used to fuck your ass, darlin'?"

"Yes, I remember everything."

"You liked it a lot."

"Hmm, I did."

He bent his head and nipped gently at her buttocks. "Want me to do it again?"

"You know I do, Master."

Zeke would be busy fixing Cantara up with the nipple clamps they'd decided upon. Raoul blindfolded her, knowing her pleasure would be enhanced by the loss of one of her senses.

"I do know it, and while I'm doing that, you think you can give Zeke one of those hum jobs of yours that you used to do so well?"

"I love the taste of Master Zeke's cock in my mouth," she breathed.

"Shit!" Zeke muttered.

* * * *

Cantara was encouraged by just how easily she had persuaded the guys to play with her. She had known they would want to, but would hold back because they were afraid she wasn't up for it again quite yet. The hell with that! She'd ridden out today, swam energetically across a lake, *and* recovered her memory. She needed to eradicate the bad times she'd been through by living life to the full. And she never felt more alive than when Raoul or Zeke was chastising her for some perceived wrongdoing.

She sighed with pleasure when Zeke fixed nipple clamps to her tits and, at the same time, Raoul's slick finger penetrated her backside. She pushed against it, desperate for more than a mere finger, well aware that the needier she became, the longer Raoul would make her wait. God, but she loved these two men! Raoul was the stereotypical tall, dark, and broodingly handsome all American boy. Zeke was swarthy, slightly mysterious and tough as they came. The two were about as different as it got in terms of background, education, and ethnicity, but they had gelled when they were on the same training program for the Green Berets and had been joined at the hip ever since.

Even though she was blindfolded, Cantara closed her eyes, the better to absorb the pleasure assaulting her from all angles. They were being gentle, by their standards. The spanking she had received had been mild, but Cantara knew better than to complain. Instead she did as they had taught her, controlled her breathing and waited for the slight stinging sensation to transmute to pleasure. The fact that she had remembered what to do and wasn't stressed by it would, she hoped, earn her a more stringent punishment the next time. She so did not want to be treated as though she was made of porcelain.

"Okay, darlin'?" Raoul asked.

"Wonderful," she replied on a long sigh.

With a tug on the nipple clamp chain, Zeke slid further beneath her and the head of his throbbing cock collided with her lips. She slid her tongue across it, reacquainting herself with his addictive taste. At the same time she was conscious of Raoul kneeling behind her and grabbing her hips. The head of his cock slid into her backside as smoothly as Cantara sucked Zeke's into her mouth. Both guys sighed at the same time—deep grunts of pleasure that Cantara would have echoed, had her mouth not been quite so comprehensively full of Zeke's hard length.

"That's it, babe," Raoul purred, slipping a little deeper, filling her backside to capacity with his throbbing prick. "Now we're fucking."

Spurred on by Raoul's passionate words, Cantara hollowed her cheeks as she sucked Zeke deeper, savoring the flavor of his arousal, earthy, sweet, and salty. Excitement flushed through her system as she started to hum and the sharp, tangible need she felt for her guys grew headier by the second. Current gathered deep in her body in response to Raoul's growing assault on her backside. A low, pulsating throb caused her to clench and tremble as her orgasm built and she tried desperately to hold it at bay.

"Shit, baby," Zeke spluttered. "You ain't lost any of your skill. Keep doing that, and I'm gonna cream your throat real good."

Raoul's loaded balls slapped against the tops of Cantara's thighs. The sensation burned and intensified, sending her sensitized body into sensory overload. It was no good, she was too close to hold back, and when Zeke reached out and played with her clit, it drove her over the edge. Desire, acute, liquid, and smoldering spiraled out of control, arousing every cell in her body, stunning her senses as blessed relief gripped her.

"Naughty!" But there was laughter in Raoul's voice as he lightly tapped her butt. "Okay, darlin', if you're back with us, let's pick this thing up."

Thinking she was probably too sensitized to be able to participate, Cantara quickly discovered just how wrong she was. Zeke was controlling the thrust of his cock in and out of her mouth just as strictly as Raoul controlled the hot, slick tempo of his thrusts into her backside. Their growing pleasure communicated itself to her. She was perspiring from a combination of hot males and her own desperation. She licked Zeke from tip to balls, sipping at his arousal and swallowing down a drop of pre-cum as turbulent heat again washed through her, flickering with the intense heat of a naked flame. Raoul slapped her butt hard and she exploded a second time. Zeke's sperm gushed into her mouth and Raoul's flooded her backside mere seconds later.

"Shit, baby," he said, pulling out of her and rolling onto his back, totally spent. "You are something else."

Zeke removed himself from her mouth and kissed her lips before also falling flat on his back, panting. Temporarily spent also, Cantara rolled into position between them and someone removed her blindfold.

"Thank you," she said in a prim voice that made them both smile. "I guess I needed that."

Chapter Thirteen

"Hey, babe." Raoul looked up from his computer screen the following morning and smiled at Cantara. "You okay?"

She walked up behind him, wrapped her arms around his neck and rested her chin on the top of his head. "Just fine."

"I just got off the phone with Sanford. He's delighted to hear you've regained your memory and wants us to take you into the hospital in Cheyenne tomorrow for some more tests."

Zeke grinned across at her. "I think he wants to write a paper for a medical journal on your symptoms, cause, and recovery. You should be charging him, darlin', not the other way around."

"I'm just glad to have my life back." She frowned. "Well kinda."

"I know what you mean, honey." Raoul covered one of her hands, resting on his shoulder. "Until we get to the bottom of this Levi business, none of us will know peace. That's what Zeke and I are looking at right now, but we just don't get it." Raoul threw down his pen in disgust. "How did Levi escape? Who's helping him, and how come we can't find out a goddamned thing about him? If we can't, with all our resources, someone powerful must be protecting him."

"This calls for a fresh perspective. Let me see."

Raoul moved aside so she could sit in his chair and read from his computer what little they had been able to find out.

"Three fucking years and we're getting nowhere," Zeke said in a disgruntled voice.

"Perhaps he's dead," Cantara suggested.

"Perhaps, but my gut says not," Raoul replied, absently playing with a strand of her hair. "You sure you're okay? No ill effects?"

"Will you stop asking me that? I've told you the last dozen times you asked that I'm fine." She paused. "Well, I would be if I could persuade you to do it again. Once isn't enough when you haven't had any for so long."

"You came twice," Zeke pointed out, grinning.

"That was last night. You guys didn't used to settle for just one round."

"No running before you can walk, sweetheart," Raoul reminded her. He lifted her from his chair, sat in it himself and settled her on his lap. "There, that's better."

"Can't argue with that," she said, leaning her head against his shoulder.

"Why don't we try coming at this another way?" Zeke suggested.

"What's on your mind, bud?" Raoul asked.

"Well, we have enough damned contacts in that part of the world. If someone's keeping him hidden, they must have a damned good reason. If we can figure out who…"

Zeke was cut off by the sound of the intercom from the adjoining barn, occupied by Mark and Karl.

"Sorry to interrupt." Mark's disembodied voice echoed through the speaker.

"No problem," Raoul replied. "What's up?"

"You're not gonna believe this, but there's a guy at the main gate who says you'll want to see him."

"This guy got a name?" Zeke asked.

"Yeah, that's the thing." Mark paused. "He says he's David Levi."

Raoul, Zeke, and Cantara gaped at one another.

"Seriously?" Raoul asked, recovering first.

"Why now, of all times?" Cantara asked no one in particular. "It has to mean something."

"We've got him on the security camera," Mark said.

Zeke headed for the screen that…well, screened all would-be visitors to the ranch. Raoul looked over his shoulder as Zeke pulled up the appropriate angle.

"Wadda you think?" Zeke asked. "Is that him?"

"He's lost weight, and he looks older," Cantara said, peering between them to take a look. "But I'd say it was him."

"And he's in the States. It was the last place we thought to look," Raoul said. "No wonder we couldn't find him. Okay, Mark. Go down to the gate, search him for weapons, and drive him back up here in your own vehicle. Let's see what the jerk has to say for himself."

A terse silence reigned while they awaited the arrival of their uninvited guest. Raoul paced the length of the room, rubbing his chin in his cupped hand as he thought it through.

"The guy's got balls, coming here, I'll give him that much," Zeke said.

"But why come now, of all times?" Raoul asked, repeating Cantara's earlier question. "I just don't get it."

"Calm down, Raoul," Cantara said, taking his hand and dragging him back to his chair. "I've had my doubts about him all along, but one thing's for sure, if he's the guilty party, he wouldn't risk coming here."

"Unless he's fed up of being a fugitive, heard about your release, darlin', and thinks he can talk us around to supporting him," Zeke said, scowling.

Raoul felt his hostility rising alone with his temper. "Good luck with that one," he muttered.

"Stop trying to second guess the poor guy and give him a chance to speak for himself," Cantara admonished. "It could just be that he's a victim in all of this, too."

"You wanna wait in the yellow room?" Raoul asked her. "This might get a little unpleasant."

"I don't need protecting, but I do want to know what's going on as much as you do. Besides, with me here you won't be able to kill the guy."

"Don't put money on it," Zeke said in a glacial tone.

They heard Mark in the entrance way and shortly after that he entered the great room with a man who, up close, was definitely Levi.

"Thanks, Mark," Zeke said.

"Shout if you need us," Mark replied, leaving them to it.

Raoul and Zeke stood protectively in front of Cantara, legs apart, arms hanging loosely at their sides, prepared for trouble, even though Levi was a shadow of the man they had once known. He had lost weight, aged ten years, and his eyes had the fixed, haunted look of a man who never stopped looking over his shoulder.

"I know what you think," he said by way of introduction, "but it wasn't me. I swear it on my children's lives."

"Let's all sit down and stop this posturing," Cantara said.

"I'm glad to see you looking well, Cantara," Levi said.

"You didn't see her a month ago." Zeke growled.

"Okay," Raoul said. "You've got our attention. Now explain why we should believe a fucking word that comes out of your lying mouth."

"Well, to start with, I had absolutely no reason to betray Cantara, or you guys, to say nothing of my country's efforts to broker peace."

"You were having an affair," Zeke replied. "Those e-mails they found on your personal computer prove it. There's not much men in your position wouldn't do to keep that secret."

"Those e-mails were planted."

"Well, of course you would say that," Raoul said, heavy on the sarcasm.

"Even if I *was* having an affair, do you think I'd be careless enough to leave the evidence where a first-year hacker could get at it? I'm way better with computers than that. It was such a clumsy plant it was almost laughable." Raoul and Zeke exchanged a look. He had a point. "I love my wife and my kids and I wanted peace in our region as much as Cantara did. Why would I sabotage her efforts?"

"You were set up?" Cantara said softly.

"Yeah, I was set up all right." He paused, looking angry and upset. "By the Americans."

Raoul and Zeke both protested.

"How do you think I broke out of jail?" he asked, making quote marks with his fingers around the words *broke out.*

Zeke aimed a lowering glare his way. "How did you?"

"I have absolutely no idea." He spread his hands and shrugged. "One minute I was in the exercise yard, being despised by my guards, the next I was on an American military plane, heading for the States. I have no recollection of how I got on it and can only assume I was given something to knock me out."

"And the guards just looked the other way?" Zeke asked skeptically.

Levi shrugged. "I was told I was an embarrassment to Israel and they didn't want what I'd done made public. So, I was being given a chance to live quietly in America *but* if I spoke out, or tried to contact my family, they would be killed and so would I."

"Who told you this?" Raoul asked.

Levi shot them a disbelieving look. "Isn't it obvious?"

"Not to us," Zeke replied.

"Pool," Levi said succinctly.

"The colonel!" Cantara breathed.

Raoul contained his own anger as he examined Levi's face for any indication that he was lying. All he could see was an overwhelming desire to finally tell his side of the story. He'd interrogated enough people to know when they were being honest, and he sensed that Levi was playing it straight. How would he have gotten out of a top security Israeli military detention center otherwise? Raoul had often wondered about that. He either worked for very powerful people opposed to peace on the West Bank, or the US Military helped him escape.

Raoul's money was on the latter.

"That bastard!" Zeke thumped the table with his clenched fist, clearly having reached the same conclusions as Raoul. "I knew there was a reason why I didn't like the jerk."

Raoul scowled. "He was on the flight with you?"

"Oh yeah. Was he ever."

"He did return stateside just after we escaped captivity," Zeke said thoughtfully. "The timing fits."

"Pool arranged my new identity and got me job as an accountant in New Jersey, which is where I've been ever since."

"If this is true, why didn't you get in touch with us before now?" Raoul asked.

"Because I knew you wouldn't believe me." He shrugged. "I know how much the two of you cared for Cantara, how devastated you were by her death. Besides, I was scared shitless, for my family more than myself. But when I heard that a woman working for the Americans had been found in a house in Palestine, I recognized you guys from the news footage shot at Andrews and knew it must be Cantara. I also figured you'd be looking for answers." He straightened his shoulders, looking more like the efficient adjutant they remembered. "I'm through with hiding, and can't live any longer with my family thinking I'm a traitor. I know it's asking a lot, but I need you to help me clear my name."

"We'll do that," Cantara said with alacrity. "Of course we will."

"What I don't understand," Zeke said, "is why Pool would do such a thing. He's an uptight prick but I never would have pegged him as a traitor."

"We've checked out his financials," Raoul added. "These things are always about money, politics or sex. He lives within his means, has modest savings, and no dirty little secrets that we could unearth. His wife is dead. Died of cancer ten years ago. He doesn't have a girlfriend and his only relatives are a married daughter and two grandkids." He shrugged. "There's nothing there. No reason on this earth why he would turn against his country."

"Have you looked into his adjutant?" Levi asked quietly.

"No," Raoul admitted. "You think Romney's the guy?"

Zeke scowled. "Even if he is, why would Pool clear up after him? I know it would make him look bad to have a traitor for an adjutant, but much as I dislike the man, I wouldn't have thought he would let that stand in the way of his fucking duty."

Levi shared an intent look between the three of them. "Perhaps it has something to do with Romney being married to his daughter," he said calmly.

* * * *

Utter astonishment greeted this statement. Cantara could tell any doubts Raoul and Zeke had harbored about Levi's version of events dissipated at that moment. It would be easy enough to check up on Romney's marital situation, so there was no point in Levi lying about it. She suspected her guys were feeling disadvantaged for not having made the connection themselves, but knew why they hadn't. They'd been grieving for her, concentrating their anger on finding Levi, and hadn't done more than a cursory check on Pool. They were usually way more efficient than that, but the strength of their feelings for her had affected their diligence.

"I'll get the guys digging into his background," Zeke said, picking up the phone.

"Tell us what you know about Romney," Raoul invited, sitting down beside Cantara and grasping her hand like a lifeline.

"To use American terminology, he's a jerk. Make that a lazy jerk. But he's very clever at hiding his inadequacies."

"I remember he's good looking," Cantara said, earning herself identical scowls from Raoul and Zeke that made her smile. She loved their possessiveness, but sometimes they took it too far.

"Oh yeah," Levi replied, "and doesn't he just know it. He turns on the charm when it suits him and fools a lot of people about his true nature, men and women alike. If anyone was having an affair, I'd put good money on it being him."

"Which would explain why Pool covered his tracks."

"Right." Levi nodded. "As a colonel he could arrange for me to be sprung from detention on some pretense or other, and get me onto a military transport plane."

"Let me put some coffee on," Cantara said, feeling on information overload and in urgent need of a shot of caffeine.

"I have a feeling Romney liked the ponies, too," Levi added. "And show me a gambler who doesn't have debts."

Cantara served coffee and they continued to mull over the question of Romney, and his motivation, while waiting for Mark and Karl to report back on their findings. They did so in person toward the end of the morning.

"Romney's constantly in debt," Jordon told them. "About the time of Cantara's abduction he was in big time with some heavy dudes who don't play nice with guys who default. Then, suddenly, there was an influx of unexplained cash into his account and his problems went away."

Raoul clenched his fists. "The bastard! Let me at him."

"Easy, partner," Zeke said, looking only fractionally less thunderous. "What else, Karl?"

"He's in deep again right now."

"Wonder who he'll betray this time to claw his way back," Raoul muttered.

"Is he still married to the colonel's daughter?" Cantara asked.

"Yeah, and their kids are in grade school."

"It has to be him," Raoul said.

"I agree," Zeke replied. "But what are we gonna do about him?"

"Other than break his fucking miserable neck, you mean?"

"Don't do that, Raoul," Cantara said, smiling sweetly. "They'll lock you up if you do."

"Even though it would be a public service?"

Cantara perched a buttock on the arm of his chair and leaned in to kiss his brow. "Even then."

"Does Colonel Hassan think you're guilty?" Zeke asked.

"Actually no, he had a real hard time with that. He told me when I went to jail that they'd soon have me out again, once they'd investigated and cleared me of any wrongdoing. He knew me well enough to accept I wouldn't cheat on my wife." Levi flashed a mirthless smile. "He also knew that if I did I was too good with computers to leave evidence of an affair in such an obvious place."

"Have you spoken to him since you arrived in the States?" Raoul asked.

"No, I was often tempted, but once I absconded I figured he would assume I was guilty, so I couldn't take the risk."

"What are you thinking?" Zeke asked Raoul.

"I'm thinking we should talk to Hassan on a secure line to start with. We know he's in this country right now, waiting to talk to Cantara."

"Wouldn't it be better to invite Agent Parker, Colonel Hassan and Colonel Pool down here?" Cantara asked. "All three of them want to talk to me. They keep ringing to ask if I've remembered anything. Tell them I now remember everything, including talk of who betrayed me that I overheard during my captivity. That ought to bring them running."

"That will be dangerous, darlin'," Raoul said, touching her hand. "I'm not taking a single risk with you again."

"If they come here to the ranch, I won't be in danger. It's home ground and you hold all the advantages since you don't let anyone past the gates if they have weapons. We can spring Mr. Levi on them and let Pool explain his way out of it."

Raoul and Zeke looked at one another. "I guess it would be the best way," Raoul said. "If we tell Hassan in advance that Levi's here, he might put duty before friendship and the next thing you know we'll be inundated with military police enforcing a search warrant."

"How do you feel about it, Levi?" Zeke asked. "There's every chance they'll throw your ass in jail first and ask questions later."

"I'm prepared to take that chance. I've had enough of living on the run."

"We'll get you fixed up with a decent lawyer, if it comes to it," Raoul said.

"Thank you. I appreciate that."

"You sure you wanna do this, babe?" Zeke asked.

Cantara nodded. "Perfectly sure." She shared a smile between her two men. "We need closure, gentlemen," she said, glancing significantly at the door to the yellow room. "I'm sure I don't need to remind you of why."

"Okay, Levi," Raoul said. "You'll be our guest until we get this sorted out. Mark and Jordon have a spare room in the barn. They'll take care of you."

"Thanks, I appreciate it." He stood up, looking resolute. "One way or another, I want my life back."

Chapter Fourteen

"It's almost over," Raoul said to Cantara the following morning. "The colonels and Parker will be here soon and we can hit them with what we know."

Cantara nodded, and reached up to cover Raoul's hand, resting on her shoulder. All three of them were on edge, excited about settling the big mystery surrounding her capture, because it would free them up to live the life they'd always envisaged for themselves. Raoul, she knew, was especially screwed up about the risks, worried the strain would be too much for her. But once the call had been placed to Parker, the die was cast. There was no turning back now. Cantara was glad. She needed closure.

I know," she replied. "Don't worry about me. I can do this. I *want* to do it."

"Do you think Pool will 'fess up, bud?" Zeke asked.

"Bet you ten bucks he doesn't."

"You're on."

Zeke prepared breakfast for the three of them, and the guys sat over Cantara, making sure she ate something. She almost elevated from her chair when the buzzer sounded, and Karl's voice came through the intercom.

"They're at the gates," he said.

"Go get 'em," Raoul replied. "You know what to do. Levi, in that room there," he added, pointing to the small den off the great room. "Keep the door closed until I come to get you."

"Good luck," Levi said.

He was grim faced and understandably tense, since his entire future hung in the balance. Even so, he managed a smile and reassuring pat on the shoulder for Cantara before leaving the room.

Cantara sat down as the wait for their visitors to reach the house seemed interminable. She caught a glimpse of her image in a nearby mirror and was shocked to see just how pale she looked. Raoul sat on the arm of her chair and played with the hairs that had escaped from her French braid. He coiled them around his index finger and brushed her nape each time he did so, sending delicious shivers down her spine that helped to distract her. Zeke sat opposite her and treated her to one of his infectiously wicked smiles as he touched her knee. They were so attuned to her needs that they always knew exactly how to make her feel better about herself.

"We got you, darlin'," they said at the same time.

"Look upon this as revenge time, and try to enjoy it," Raoul said alone. "You've sure as hell earned the right."

"I'm okay, really."

"We'll make you feel more than okay later, sweetheart," Zeke said, winking at her. "Hold that thought."

"You have to do whatever I want you to?" she asked, widening her eyes.

"Oh no, darlin'." Raoul's predatory smile, full of innuendo and self-assurance, caused her pulse to quicken and her pussy to spring a leak faster than the national debt. Damn it, now wasn't the time, but when he looked at her that way, her body played by its own rules and she simply couldn't help the way she responded to his flirtatious challenges. "You know better than that. We're in charge in the yellow room and if you make demands it'll earn you a good, hard spanking."

A gurgle of laughter slipped past her guard. "Will it now?"

"Witch!"

Raoul didn't have a chance to do anything other than tap her thigh before they heard the door open and voices in the vestibule.

"Game on," Zeke muttered, standing.

The three men strode into the room, Agent Parker in the lead, and shook hands with Raoul and Zeke. From her chair Cantara could see just how hard it was for her two guys to shake Pool's hand without detaching it from his wrist. All three of them then turned to look at her, smiles plastered on their faces.

"So pleased to hear you're better," Parker said, sounding sincere.

"Thanks, yes. I feel much better." She motioned to the seats surrounding her. "Forgive me if I don't get up. But please, sit down, all of you. How can I help you?"

"If it's not too painful, talk us through everything that happened to you."

Cantara did so, and for the most part no one interrupted her. Occasionally Parker asked for clarification on some point or other, but aside from that, the floor was Cantara's.

"Can you remember the names of any of the people who stopped by to talk to Salim?" Parker asked.

Cantara could, and gave them, along with descriptions and as much as she knew about each individual's background. Parker was recording everything she said, but still took copious notes.

Pool, who looked distinctly unwell, broke his silence. "Did you hear anything said about Levi's reasons for turning traitor?" he asked.

"How could she have done?" Raoul replied for her. "Since you know as well as I do that Levi wasn't the traitor."

Hassan looked surprised. Parker, significantly, did not, and Cantara wondered just how much information the spook was privy to that he wasn't sharing. Pool fell back on belligerence and posturing.

"What the devil do you mean by that remark, Washington?" Pool stood up, as pugnacious as ever, but Raoul and Zeke stood also, making him appear puny and insignificant by comparison. "Levi's e-mails condemned him, to say nothing of his breaking out of jail."

"Those e-mails were planted," Zeke replied. "And he didn't break out of the detention center. He was removed by the US military to be taken back to headquarters for questioning."

"What's all this?" Hassan asked, sending Pool a questioning glare.

"We know the truth, Pool," Raoul said. "You have one chance to help yourself and confess, and this is it."

"I know you don't like me, Washington, and I can assure you the feeling's mutual. Just because you aren't as good as you think you are and managed to lose your wife, don't blame me for your incompetence."

"Told you he wouldn't man-up," Raoul said, shrugging. "You owe me ten bucks, bud."

"Americans soldiers went to the detention center with a signed order to release Levi to them so he could be taken for questioning," Zeke said. "Who do you suppose signed that order, Pool?"

The colonel shrugged. "How would I know?"

"It was signed by your adjutant, and countersigned by you."

"Bullshit!"

"Is it?" Raoul asked, flexing a brow.

He strolled about the room, hands clasped behind his back, clearly enjoying himself. Cantara enjoyed watching him. In spite of all those rippling muscles and his aura of tightly controlled strength, his movements were lithe and graceful—a flowing display of masculine vitality that she would have to be dead not to appreciate, no matter how lousy and inappropriate the timing of her thoughts. But it was always that way whenever she was anywhere near Zeke and Raoul. However dire the situation, sex was never far from her thoughts, and she had long since learned not to fight against the power of her instincts. The feel of their hands doing what they did so well, the exquisite agony of being chastised by one or both of them, the joy when they finally penetrated her...

Dear God, she was damp again. Cantara opened her eyes wide and made a superhuman effort to pull her thoughts away from the erotic direction they appeared determined to take. She blamed her guys for that, of course. How was she supposed to concentrate on the matter in hand when they kept distracting her with displays of raw musculature? Anyway, Raoul was right. They had earned this moment and she intended to make the most of it.

"I had a feeling that's what you would say," Raoul said, "and so I called in a few favors." Had he? That was news to Cantara. Raoul leaned over his desk and extracted a piece of paper from a drawer, winked at her and handed the paper to Parker. "This is a copy of the order in question."

Hassan leaned over Parker's shoulder and read it. "This says Levi was required for joint questioning by the task force. My name's cited, but I knew nothing about this."

"Because the questioning would never take place," Zeke replied. "It was a ruse to break Levi out of custody because the real traitor knew the evidence he'd planted wouldn't hold up. He screwed up there, not being as proficient at computer hacking. Levi could have proven he wasn't having an affair, and even if there was still any doubt, no one who knew him would ever believe he'd left evidence laying around where anyone could find it. You didn't believe it, did you, colonel?" Zeke asked, addressing the comment to Hassan.

"No, not for one moment, but when it looked like he had absconded, I no longer knew what to think."

"Which is precisely why it was made to appear as though he'd gone on the run. Guilt by association."

"I knew nothing about this, either," Pool said, sounding rather desperate. "I didn't sign that order."

"Yeah, you did, but you weren't the traitor."

"Romney," Hassan hissed.

"Exactly right, colonel. We would have put it together sooner, but for the fact that we didn't know he was married to Pool's daughter."

The air left Pool's lungs in an extravagant whoosh and he fell back into his chair.

"You kept that one quiet," Hassan said, clearly seething.

"You knew Romney hadn't covered his tracks well enough to fool anyone for long, and so cleaned up for him. I suspect not for the first time," Raoul said.

"Why did Romney do it?" Parker asked.

"He was badly in debt to some very unforgiving people," Zeke replied. "We have his financials that show those debts mysteriously disappeared shortly after Cantara did." He fixed Parker with a significant look. "But I'm probably not telling you anything you didn't already know."

"It's all circumstantial," Pool blustered. "If Levi's so innocent, why doesn't he step forward?"

"My thoughts precisely," Raoul said, opening the door to the den, through which Levi walked, shoulders back, head held high.

"Hello, Colonel," he said, offering his hand to Hassan.

Hassan grasped it in both of his and then engulfed Levi in a back-slapping hug. "Why didn't you contact me?" he asked.

Levi explained all that had happened to him, and the part Pool had played in it. Especially the threats against his family.

"Which is why I couldn't take the risk," he finished. "Until I heard Cantara was safe. Then I came here, hoping Washington and Orion would hear me out before killing me, which they did."

"It's his word against mine," Pool said. "A distinguished colonel—"

"Distinguished?" Zeke threw Pool a disbelieving look.

"A distinguished colonel with a spotless record against an adjutant who can't keep his pecker in his pants."

Raoul smiled at Pool's bluster. "Once Romney's been picked up and interrogated, his financials soured, my guess is, we'll soon know who's telling the truth." He held Pool in a death glare. "Sure you wanna go there? There's still time to distance yourself."

Pool appeared to shrink in his chair and suddenly looked years older as he dropped his head into his hand, clearly realizing he couldn't bluster his way out of this one.

"We've pieced it all together," Zeke said, "but would like to hear it from you, Colonel."

No one spoke, but every pair of eyes in the room was trained condemningly upon Pool.

"Everything I've done has been done to protect my daughter," he said in a defeated voice. "I want you to believe that. She and her kids are the only people I have left in the world worth living for. I warned her against Romney when she first started dating him. There was something about him I didn't trust, but she was smitten and there was nothing I could do to stop them from marrying." He looked up and grimaced. "She's still smitten, by the way. No matter how badly he treats her, she stands by him. I've lost count of the number of times I've offered to look after her and the kids, but she won't even consider leaving him."

"And so when he didn't meet the criteria for any of the elite corps he wanted to become a part of, you got him a job close to you where you could keep an eye on him?" Zeke suggested.

"Pretty much."

"How could you cover up for him when you knew he'd probably gotten me killed, and could easily have gotten Raoul and Zeke killed, too?" Cantara demanded to know. "You swore an oath, didn't you?"

Pool spread his hands. "You were determined to go in there. Your brother-in-law would have gotten you, no matter what. I don't condone what Romney did, in fact I nearly broke his damned neck when I found out. But in the end, all he did was tell those people you and Washington were married."

Raoul shook his head. "I can't believe your stupidity, although I suppose it shouldn't surprise me. Salim was obsessed with Cantara. When he found out she'd married me, it tipped him over the edge with jealousy. She suffered way more at his hands because of that *and* because he knew we had her back, he was able to lay a trap for us."

"We would have been able to get her away from Salim, if we'd followed her as planned and knew where she'd been taken," Zeke added in disgust.

"Yes," Pool said in a tired voice. "I don't doubt it for a moment. I just haven't wanted to admit it to myself."

"You need to turn yourself in, Pool," Raoul said. "It will be easier on you if you do that."

"I'll put arrangements in hand to have Romney picked up," Parker said. "He still works for Pool, but at the Pentagon now."

"Just don't let him anywhere near us," Raoul growled.

"A ruined career for a louse who didn't deserve it and a daughter with no self-respect," Zeke muttered as Agent Parker escorted Pool from the ranch.

"Do you have a secure outside line?" Hassan asked.

Raoul flexed a brow. "What do you think?" he replied, handing Hassan the handset.

"Who's he calling?" Cantara asked as Raoul sat beside her and took her hand.

"Shush, just watch."

"Rachel?" Hassan asked, ignoring Levi's gasp. "It's Colonel Hassan. How are you? Just fine, thanks. I'm in the States right now and there's someone here who needs to talk to you."

With tears pouring down his face, David Levi took the receiver from Hassan with a shaking hand and spoke to the wife he adored for the first time in three years.

Chapter Fifteen

That afternoon, Raoul and Zeke drove Cantara into Cheyenne for her appointment at the hospital.

"It's a pretty drive," Cantara said, watching the passing scenery from her position sandwiched between the guys on the bench seat of their truck.

"That it is, darlin'," Zeke agreed, but he was looking at Cantara, not the view.

"Nature on steroids this time of year," Raoul agreed.

He would be looking at Cantara, too, if he hadn't been driving. He still sneaked frequent peaks in her direction whenever the road was clear. He didn't seem able to stop looking at her, just to convince himself they really did have her back. This time for keeps.

He pulled into the hospital parking lot and it wasn't long before the three of them were ushered into Sanford's consulting rooms. A nurse checked Cantara's vital signs and then said Dr. Sanford would be right with them.

"Well, Cantara," Sanford said, striding into the room a short time later, beaming as though he took personal credit for her recovery. "I hear it's good news."

"It certainly is," she replied, shaking his outstretched hand.

"You look much better than when I saw you last."

She bit her lip, presumably to prevent herself from explaining what had put the sparkle back in her eye. Wouldn't do to frighten the horses, Raoul thought, stifling a smile of his own. He caught Cantara's eye and flashed her a warning look. He didn't want to think what mischief she might be capable of causing when she got that devilish look in her eye. He knew her game. She was trying to earn herself punishment credits. He shook his head, full of admiration for his feisty wife's ability to bounce back with spirit and verve so soon after her ordeal.

To Raoul's relief and her evident amusement, she told Sanford how everything had come flooding back, thanks to a throwaway comment he had made.

"That's just great. Sometimes that's all it takes. Recollection by association. The psychologists call it disassociation, which is what happened to you. Your conscious mind protected itself by retreating to a safe place to survive the trauma of your captivity. Do you want to tell me what happened to you, or aren't you ready to talk about it yet?"

"I don't mind telling you."

She gave an abridged, sanitized version of her suffering at the hands of her delusional brother-in-law. Raoul grasped her hand and squeezed it encouragingly, figuring Sanford must know what he was doing in getting her talking about it.

"No wonder your mind couldn't cope," he said matter-of-factly. "But I'm glad to see you don't seem to be permanently damaged by your ordeal." *How the fuck can he be so sure?* "Now then, I want to take some blood, run some more tests, and get you to have another CAT scan, just to make absolutely sure we haven't missed anything, if that's okay with you."

Cantara shrugged. "Sure, but I feel fine."

"No more headaches?"

"Well, it's early days yet. I only recovered my memory a couple of days ago, but so far there have been none."

"Okay then, let's get this done."

The blood was taken, then the nurse asked Cantara to follow her. "She'll not be long," she told the guys.

"No problem. We'll be in the waiting room," Zeke replied.

* * * *

Cantara was taken to a cubicle where she was invited to strip off and don the ubiquitous hospital gown. Once she had done so, the nurse told her to take a seat in the anti-room and that someone would be right with her. Another gowned woman sat there, flipping through a magazine as she waited. She and Cantara nodded to one another—kindred spirits in unflattering clothing—but didn't speak. An orderly popped his head around the door and called the other woman.

"I'll be right back for you, ma'am," he said to Cantara. "You're our last victim this morning."

Cantara smiled at the guy's feeble attempt at humor, then sat twiddling her thumbs, not surprised when he didn't come back immediately. Hospitals ran to their own timescales. She filled the time thinking about the events of the past twenty-four hours, nervous about the arrival of the military that afternoon, but anxious to get it over and done with. Levi had suffered almost as badly as she had. More so in some respects since she knew she was placing herself in danger when she volunteered for the role of go-between. Levi was simply doing his job. It must be the worst thing in the world to be separated from his family, to miss his children growing up, to have them think he was a traitor. She really hoped they could fix things for him—to say nothing of themselves.

She hugged herself when she thought about all the things she and the guys got up to in the yellow room. They had spanked her again last night, then tied her up and took turns to fuck her until every bone in her body felt gloriously liquefied. She wanted them both at once, but Raoul, in his infinite wisdom, decreed she wasn't strong enough yet. Cantara harrumphed and straightened her shoulders. She was perfectly willing to play submissive but hell would freeze over before either of them told her what she was or was not strong enough to attempt.

"Come on," she muttered, when the waiting appeared to stretch on forever.

As she said it, the door opened behind her and an orderly in scrubs came into the room, but not the same one as before. She gathered up her purse but barely looked at him, until she heard the door lock click behind him. Her scalp prickled as she slowly looked into his face. She recognized him immediately.

It was Romney, and this was clearly not a social visit.

"You're supposed to be dead," he said accusingly.

"Sorry to disappoint you."

Cantara was astonished when her voice sounded so level when her heart was pounding, and her pulse was racing out of control. At least the nagging feeling she'd been wrestling with all day now made sense. Why hadn't they stopped to consider he might not be at the Pentagon? Because they hadn't thought he would be stupid, or desperate enough, to come anywhere near her, Cantara supposed.

"How did you know I would be here?" she asked.

"I figured you'd run to your doctor just as soon as you got your memory back." He shrugged. "I hacked into his appointments calendar and struck pay dirt."

"You won't get away with whatever you're planning to do. We know it was you who set Levi up, and then got daddy-in-law to clean up for you."

"Aw, he didn't need to do that. Far as I was concerned, Levi could go down for the crime and that would be that."

"You didn't plant convincing enough evidence against him."

He did a one-shouldered shrug this time, arms folded across a disconcertingly solid-looking chest. "Where there's smoke there's fire."

"You didn't stop to think they might look at you next?"

"Your boyfriends didn't." He chuckled. "All this time, they've been fretting about what happened to you, chasing their tails trying to find Levi, and didn't once think it could be me."

"They think so now. So Does Agent Parker and Colonel Hassan. You won't get away. They're looking for you."

"That's okay. They won't look here, but if you'd stayed dead, or at least brain-dead, it would have saved us both a heap of trouble." He waved a syringe in the air and grabbed her arm. "Now don't make a fuss. This will send you to sleep, no pain." He giggled like a girl. "You'll like it, trust me on this."

Shit, she was in trouble! He was twice her size and strength, *and* he had a damned good reason to want her dead.

"You can't kill everyone involved," she said in a reasonable tone. "Raoul and Zeke know everything I remembered."

"Hearsay," he said dismissively.

"Not if Colonel Pool testifies against you."

"He won't do that." But Romney sounded a little less sure of himself. "He always puts his daughter ahead of everything else, and his daughter worships the ground I walk on."

"Don't count on it."

She wanted to tell him they had Levi but if she mentioned him, would he give it up and disappear? Most likely not, but the only alternative was to die, here and now. It had to be worth a shot.

"How do you think we found out the truth?" she asked.

He fixed her with a chilling look. "Like I give a shit."

"We have Levi." His head shot up and his grip on her arm momentarily loosened, but not enough for her to break free. Even if she did, the door was locked. She would never get past his bulk. "Pool brought him to the States, got him a new identity, a job, and he can prove it."

"Really!" He quirked a brow. "Too bad, but I shall instigate plan B and disappear after I've dealt with you. Shame that, I was hoping to build a bigger nest egg first, but Pool's daughter is becoming a real nag. It's time to move on to a younger model, as they say."

"If you're leaving, there's no need to kill me and have a murder charge hanging over your head. Raoul and Zeke will figure out it was you and will hunt you down."

He chuckled, a manic sound that chilled Cantara's blood. "They haven't done too good a job of finding me so far."

"They know who they're looking for now. You'd never be able to stop looking over your shoulder, especially since the military now has a warrant out for your arrest."

"Touching of you to care, but I'll take my chances, thanks all the same."

Hell, he really meant to do this. There had to be something she could do to help herself. She used to be able to get the better of men his size, but was still weak and out of practice in hand-to-hand combat. Where the heck was the real orderly? Was there a panic button she could reach? She saw the large red button in question on the opposite wall, tantalizingly just out of her reach. She delved into her purse behind her back with her free hand and searched frantically for the cell phone Raoul had given her. Who was the last person she'd called on it? *Think, Cantara, think!*

It had to be one of the guys. Who else would she call? Yes, it was Zeke. He was in the paddock the previous afternoon, lunging Iesha, and Cantara had rang him to see if he needed anything. Trusting to luck that she hit the right button on a phone she wasn't used to and couldn't actually look at, she pressed last number redial. She barely had time to do so before Romney jerked her to her feet, his grip vicious, unbreakable.

"Such a shame," he muttered, putting his face up close to hers. "I always did have the hots for you, but there's no time to do anything about it now. They'll be wondering why you haven't turned up for your scan."

"Where's the orderly who should have collected me?" she asked, speaking as loud as she dared, hoping she was getting through to Zeke.

"Oh, tied up in a cupboard. He'll survive which, unfortunately, is more than can be said for you."

* * * *

"They're taking their sweet time," Zeke remarked, flipping through a gun magazine.

Raoul yawned and stretched his arms above his head. "Yeah well, I expect they're backed up as usual."

"I still don't get how we didn't figure Romney for the traitor. It's kinda obvious, when you think about it."

"Not so very obvious," Raoul replied. "I hate to admit it, but he fooled me. Perhaps because we were always at odds with Pool and Romney went out of his way to smooth things over for us."

"Jerk!"

"Yeah well, at least we now know—"

Zeke's cell phone beeped. "You're supposed to turn that thing off in here."

Zeke shot him a look, checked the caller display and jerked upright. "It's Cantara."

"What!"

They listened and heard Cantara asking what had happened to the real orderly.

"Something's wrong," Raoul said tersely.

Both men threw themselves from their chairs and ran in the direction of the CAT scan room. They asked the astonished receptionist where Cantara was and raced toward the room she indicated.

"You can't go in there," she called after them.

Raoul tried the door, but it was locked. Without a second's thought he stood back, raised his foot and gave the lock a hefty kick. The door flew open and crashed against the inside wall, sending chunks of partitioning flying in the air. Raoul's heart lurched when he saw Cantara losing her struggle with Romney. He had a syringe in his hand and was trying to inject her with its contents. Their arrival didn't seem to faze him in the least and he increased his efforts to subdue Cantara, who was kicking, gouging and putting up one hell of a fight.

The problem was, Romney was holding her too close for her blows to have much impact. Something needed to be done about that, but with that needle so close to her arm, Raoul couldn't risk moving in and breaking Romney's miserable neck, which every cell in his body urged him to do. If he did that, Romney would have ample time to inject Cantara with whatever deadly concoction he had in that syringe before Raoul and Zeke could save her. He drew in several shuddering breaths, forcing himself to calm down and assess the situation dispassionately. He had been trained to disassociate himself emotionally in tight situations and had never had a more compelling reason to employ that talent.

"You're a dead man, Romney," Zeke said, his murderous expression so intent that even Raoul was intimidated by it. No one with an ounce of sense fucked with Zeke when he was in such an uncompromising mood. "Let her go."

"Not a chance. If I'm dead, I'm taking her with me." He smirked. "Not quite so tough now are you, assholes?"

"Is that your problem, Romney?" Raoul taunted. "You wanted to be one of the best but didn't have the balls to make the grade, so you got daddy-in-law to fix you up with a nice safe desk job. But deep down inside you know you're a coward, which means you have a grudge against the world and take out your frustrations on defenseless women." Raoul shook his head as he continued to goad the creep. "That must make you feel like you actually have stones."

"You don't know shit about me."

But Raoul's words had the desired effect. While focusing his attention on Raoul, he momentarily loosened his hold on Cantara, affording her the opportunity she needed. Raoul could only watch, impotent, hoping she would understand what he had done and be quick enough to take advantage. He exchanged a proud smile with Zeke as he observed what happened next, wondering how he could ever have doubted her.

"Just so we're clear," she said, "there's absolutely nothing defenseless about me."

Before Romney could transfer his attention to her, Cantara demonstrated her point by using the additional space now separating them to bring up her knee and deploy it in Romney's groin with enough force to make even Raoul's eyes water. Attagirl! The bastard had it coming. She followed up that move with a sharp chop to his windpipe with the side of her hand—a move which he and Zeke had taught her in a previous life. It saw the syringe fly from his hand and clatter to the floor. Romney, puce in the face and struggling to breathe, howled and slowly crumpled to his knees. He curled into a defensive ball as he nursed his damaged genitalia, but had the foresight to roll quickly out of the range of Raoul's rapidly approaching feet. Unfortunately for him, that meant he landed right on top of the syringe.

"This is getting to be a habit," Cantara said in a shrill voice, presumably thinking of the time when she had dealt with Salim in a similar fashion.

"Babe, are you okay?" Raoul caught her just before her knees buckled beneath her.

"I obviously haven't forgotten how to kick ass," she replied with a feeble smile.

"Thank God you had the presence of mind to call me," Zeke said, moving in for a hug. "If I'd obeyed the rules and switched my phone off—"

"I was counting on you not having done so," Cantara replied as Raoul helped her to a chair. She was trembling so badly that he refused to let her go, even when she was seated. If this episode caused her any setbacks then Raoul wouldn't be responsible for his actions.

"I'm gonna cause one hell of a stink with the hospital administrators over this," he said, grinding his jaw as he continued to hold Cantara in a protective embrace, sensing her trembles slowly decreasing. "This is the one place where you ought to have been safe on your own."

"We should have figured he'd get worried when word leaked that Cantara had regained her memory," Zeke said, checking Romney to ensure he had a pulse. "Unfortunately, he's still alive."

"He hacked into Dr. Sanford's appointment book," Cantara said.

"What's going on?"

Hospital security belatedly streamed into the room, closely followed by Sanford, who appeared both harried and horrified. He checked Romney for himself, then started barking orders to his hovering underlings.

"You were lucky, Cantara," Sanford said grimly when Romney, unconscious and with a drip attached to his arm, was gurneyed from the room.

"I'm calling the sheriff," Zeke said, watching him go and pulling his cell phone from his pocket. "He can't be allowed to leave."

"He won't be going anywhere," Sanford replied. "Whatever he was trying to inject Cantara with, some of it got into his system when he fell on the needle and it pierced his skin. His weight on the syringe itself must have somehow forced the liquid into him."

"Not enough if he's still alive," Zeke groused.

"We're running some tests to identify what it was so we can treat him."

"Strychnine is my guess," Raoul said, scowling. "Bastard! How the hell did he get in here without anyone noticing?"

"It's not a prison. People come and go all the time. Staff rotate." Sanford sounded defensive. "I probably shouldn't say anything more and refer you to our legal people, just in case you decide to sue the hospital for which, off the record, I wouldn't blame you."

"You're safe. We deal with our problems our way," Zeke replied, his tone silk on steel, as he hung up on the local sheriff. "But you might wanna adjust your bill, seeing as how—"

"Zeke!" Cantara punched his arm. "It's not Dr. Sanford's fault."

"Hmm," was Raoul's only response.

"Come on, guys," Cantara said. "Take me home. We're expecting visitors this afternoon, don't forget, and I can't wait to help Levi clear his name."

"After you've had your scan," Raoul replied, brushing his knuckles softly down the side of her face. "That's what we came here to do and that low life ain't gonna stop us."

Chapter Sixteen

An hour later they were back in the truck. Cantara finally had her scan, but Raoul and Zeke refused to wait outside the room or leave her alone for a single second. Cantara wouldn't admit it but she was grateful for their protectiveness. The incident with Romney had shaken her badly, probably because she wasn't firing on all cylinders again quite yet. She felt cold, in spite of the warmth of the day, and was forced to lace her fingers together in her lap so the guys couldn't see her hands shaking and worry about her more than they already did.

"At least Romney's under guard," Zeke said with satisfaction. "I've given Parker a call. He's sending people to pick him up."

"That I would pay good money to see," Raoul replied.

"No need. This one's on the house." Zeke slid an arm around Cantara and kissed her hair. She gratefully rested her head on his broad shoulder and closed her eyes as tiredness seeped through her. "You okay, darlin'?" he asked.

"I've had better days," she replied, still with her eyes closed. "But at least we got the bad guy and the danger's gone."

"Yeah," Raoul replied from behind the wheel. "It's finally over."

"We should have anticipated that Romney would pitch up here," Zeke growled. "We left you exposed again, darlin'. That ain't acceptable."

"What he said," Raoul added, grimacing. "We're the ones who put it about that Cantara had regained her memory. We didn't stop to think that Romney would have time to come up with a plan to ambush her and expect to get away with it."

"He might have done," Cantara said, shuddering. "If he'd injected me and I collapsed, everyone would assume it was something to do with my treatment. Some allergic reaction, or something like that. By the time the truth came out, he would have been long gone."

"Even so, we thought he would be more likely to do a runner," Zeke said.

"Good job I've had practice kneeing men in the balls."

Cantara's comment earned her scowls from Raoul and Zeke and her attempt to lighten the mood fell flat.

"What will happen to Pool and Romney?" Cantara asked.

"None of this will come out," Zeke warned her. "You need to be ready for that. It would be a disaster for Israeli-American relations, and would spell disaster for the negotiations with the Palestinians."

"That's not fair!"

"No, darlin', it ain't," Raoul agreed, squeezing her shoulders. "But it's why Parker was so closely involved. I always suspected he knew more than he was letting on, and he was here to make sure none of it got into the public domain."

Cantara widened her eyes. "He knew Levi wasn't the traitor?"

"He probably suspected it," Zeke replied. "And once you resurfaced, it was just a matter of waiting to see if you regained your memory, and what shook loose. Course, they didn't count on Levi showing himself, which could have been a bit awkward if Parker hadn't been around to smooth ruffled feathers."

"Pool and Romney, at best, will get dishonorable discharges on some pretext or other," Raoul said, curling his upper lip in evident disdain.

"They deserve way worse than that," Cantara protested.

"For Pool, nothing could be worse," Zeke assured her. "His reputation will be in tatters, his old comrades will shun him, and that will be a living death for him. As for Romney, I imagine Pool's daughter will finally see the light and ditch the bastard. I have a feeling they'll find a reason to lock him up for a while, too."

"Anyway, it's over." Raoul sent Cantara a sinfully enticing smile that left her in no doubt about the nature of his thoughts. "At last we can get on with our lives."

Cantara closed her eyes and sighed. "It was so lovely to see Levi after he spoke with his wife. Only to think, she never doubted him, even though she hadn't seen or spoken to him for three years. Can you imagine the stigma she's had to live with, but she never gave up on him. That's true love."

"There's nothing you can teach us about true love," Raoul said in a tone that brooked no argument. "We never stopped loving you, even though we thought you were dead."

"We tried to move on with our lives, but you're an impossible act to follow," Zeke added, swooping in to steal a kiss.

"You guys are so sweet." Cantara swiped away tears with the back of her hand. "For my part, I don't care what Sanford says, but no one can convince me I lost my memory because of a stupid fractured skull. I lost it when I saw that picture of you guys dead. It was too much for me to take on board, I couldn't stand the agony of losing something so precious to me, to say nothing of the guilt, so my mind shut down."

"Tonight we start living again," Raoul said, tightening his hold on her and kissing the top of her head. "Come on, darlin', you look beat. I'm gonna run you a nice hot bath. Take a long soak and when you come out, Zeke and I will have a celebration dinner ready."

"That sounds like a plan."

"I'll leave the clothes you're to wear for us laid out on the bed," Zeke added. "We don't expect to see you again for an hour and a half."

She moistened her lips and smiled at each of them in turn. "Whatever you say, gentlemen. I know better than to argue with you."

Zeke choked on a laugh. "Is that so?"

"Of course," she replied innocently. "But before we get down to playing, I need to know what I can do to help you guys around here."

"What do you mean?" Zeke asked suspiciously. "I hope you're not thinking of going back to Palestine because I gotta tell you—"

"No, at least not yet." She chewed her lower lip. "But you know me well enough to know I'm not the type to sit around twiddling my thumbs. I need something worthwhile to do."

"When you're fully recovered," Raoul said, scowling.

"Of, of course."

"Well, when you are, we'll talk about you helping with the agency work. Zeke and I take on cases ourselves sometimes."

"Yeah, it might be good, the three of us working together again."

"Just so long as you don't give me all the safe, easy jobs," she warned.

"We don't take any of those," Zeke assured her.

"Just as well, because I think I've proved I can still kick ass."

"That you have, darlin'. That you have."

Laughing, Raoul led her by the hand into the huge en-suite attached to the yellow room. He turned on the taps and poured half a bottle of fragrant oil into the steaming bath water. He lit aromatherapy candles and set them in holders around the tub. Zeke appeared and placed a large glass of white wine on the bath surround. Soothing music played through the built-in speakers.

"There you go, darlin'," Raoul said, helping her out of her clothes and into the tub.

She sighed with pleasure as she sank into the sudsy water, leaned back and closed her eyes, feeling as though a huge weight had been lifted from her shoulders. She heard the guys walk quietly from the room and close the door softly behind them, but didn't even have the energy to say good-bye.

Cantara half dozed in the bath and allowed her mind to wander. They had gotten to the truth behind her abduction, were all together again, and had another chance to live. One that Cantara had no intention of squandering with misguided good intentions this time. She understood what had driven her lovers to strive for the truth. They felt they had let her down and, as men of action and resolve, allowing the perpetrators to get away unscathed would have eaten away at them like a virulent disease. They would not have found real peace. But now, it was done and nothing stood in the way of their being together, in every sense of the word.

The atmosphere had sizzled with anticipation ever since Levi and Hassan left and Cantara realized they had suggested she indulge herself for reasons other than her being tired. They were planning something. Tonight they would finally get their relationship back on course and nothing would be taboo. She sure as hell hoped not, she thought, as she vigorously soaped her pussy. She recalled with absolute clarity the things they had done to her before they had left for the ill-fated trip to Israel and her recovery would not be complete, until they did them again.

All of them. Repeatedly.

Her wine glass was empty, the water starting to cool. Reluctantly, Cantara stood up and switched on the overhead shower to wash the shampoo from her hair. She climbed from the tub, dried herself off and brushed out her wet hair.

"Wonder what they expect me to wear," she speculated aloud, and she wandered into the bedroom. "Oh my!"

She clapped a hand over her mouth to stifle a laugh when she saw the garment, such as it was, that they had lain out on the bed. Just one garment—underwear would obviously be surplus to requirements this evening—and a pair of shoes with five-inch heels.

"What do we have here?"

She picked up what appeared to be a honeycomb fishnet dress, with a halter neck and hemline that would finish halfway down her thighs. With a giggle and a shrug she pulled it over her head and looked in the mirror with a combination of curiosity and trepidation. She hadn't regained enough weight to do this…er, dress justice. Had she?

Hmm, perhaps it didn't look too bad. Her nipples had hardened in anticipation and peeked through the holes in the fishnet. She could even see the pink lips of her pussy, which she figured was the idea. She felt sexy in a tarty sort of way, especially when she added shoes that made her legs seem endless.

She returned to the bathroom, dried her hair so that it tumbled down her back in a disorderly array of curls, gave her eyelashes a quick flick of mascara and her lips a slash of gloss. She examined her reflection again, unsurprised to notice her eyes gleaming with anticipation and her cheeks flushed deep pink for the same reason.

"Okay, bring it on," she said to the sexy image starting back at her.

She took a deep breath and headed for the great room. It was now dark outside and they had followed the theme through from the bathroom by lighting candles on every available surface, creating a romantic ambience. A bowl of fragrant roses sat in the center of the table, giving off a heady perfume. Leave it to her guys to think of flowers. The table itself was set with crisp white linen, sparkling crystal glasses, and china she had never seen before. The same background music spilled from the speakers and a log fire burned in the grate. It wasn't strictly necessary. The evenings tended to be cool, it was true, but the nature of Cantara's thoughts already had her overheating.

"Hey, guys. Something smells nice. What's for dinner?"

* * * *

"Fucking hell!" Raoul glanced away from the hob, where he was stirring his sauce, and looked his fill at Cantara instead. Shit, she was red hot! That dress was a sensation. He thought so and so did his cock, which stood to rigid attention. No change there then. "Hello, darlin'," he said, sending her a wicked smile.

"What he said," Zeke agreed. "Let's get you another glass of wine."

Zeke poured her wine and steered her to the seating area. Raoul left his sauce to simmer, grabbed beers for him and Zeke, and went to join them.

"You look…er, refreshed," he said, blowing Cantara a kiss. "You asked what was for dinner and I reckon it could just be you. Dressed like that you are definitely messing with our plans, 'cause I'm pretty sure I can't wait until afterwards."

"Mr. Control Freak has met his limit," Cantara said, laughing at him. "I never thought that day would dawn."

"I'd need to be a fucking monk not to be affected by you in that get up."

"True, but something's missing." Zeke canted his head and examined her critically. "Nipple clamps," he decided. "I'll be right back."

"I have to wear nipple clamps all through dinner?"

"You have to do as you're told. Speaking of which, come here."

Raoul patted his knee and she elegantly rose from her chair and sashayed across the room in her tall heels to join him. She plonked herself on his lap and wrapped her arms around his neck.

"Feels like you're pleased to see me," she said, giggling as she wiggled around, inflicting severe damage on his erection.

"You have no idea."

"Oh, I think I get the picture. I feel the same way. Now that we're free to be ourselves, I feel…well, de-mob happy."

"Good phraseology." Raoul slid his hands beneath her butt and lifted him from his lap. He unsnapped his jeans and unzipped, freeing his pulsating erection. "Straddle my knees, sweetheart. I need a little taster."

With the fingers of one hand, he eased his path of entry and slid the tip of his cock into her. Feeling no need to take things gently, he thrust himself all the way home with one powerful flex of his hips, filling her with his desperate need. At the same time he latched his teeth onto one of the solidified nipples that peeped through the honeycomb fabric and bit down. She threw her head back, eyes wide open, and cried out.

"Yeah, you like that, don't you, sugar? You can't get enough of my cock, or Zeke's. You're gonna wear the pair of us out with your needs."

He thrust with even more force, bit her nipple harder, and slapped her butt with one free hand. Raoul was on fire with need, and in no mood to practice restraint. He could sense Cantara was similarly minded and increased the harsh tempo of his upward motions, stretching the tight walls of her cunt to the absolute limit with his throbbing cock.

"You are gonna come so many times tonight, darlin', that you probably won't be able to walk straight tomorrow."

"I need you and Zeke to bring me back to life, Master," she replied, panting as she rode his cock like a woman emerging from a three-year sex drought. "Whatever you need, I'll stay with you."

"I know you will. This is just an appetizer, and it's gonna be quick." Raoul circled his butt against the seat as he thrust hard and deep, feeling her closing the walls of her pussy around his length as though afraid he might take it away from her. "That's it, darlin'. Let's really fuck."

The exploded together. Cantara's cries, loud and uninhibited as she orgasmed, were music to Raoul's ears. He worked her into a frenzy before he finished coming himself, and then kissed her long and deep, never wanting to let her go.

"Couldn't wait for me, huh?" Zeke asked, watching them with an amused expression, nipple clamps dangling negligently from the fingers of one hand.

Raoul laughed. "It's our little sub's fault for being so goddamned sexy. She steals away my self-control."

"You've never had any where she's concerned."

Raoul shrugged. "True. Go grab a cloth from the bathroom, bud."

"I'm on it."

Raoul cuddled Cantara close until Zeke returned. He then slid out of her and sat her back on the settee, legs spread and a satiated expression on her lovely face as Zeke gently wiped her clean. Once he'd done so, he carefully attached the nipple clamps, leaving them on the outside of the honeycomb dress, linked together by a chain.

"Just perfect," Zeke said. "Now go finish preparing dinner and leave me to have some quality time with our little gal."

"Play nice without me, guys," Raoul said, tweaking the nipple clamp chain and taking himself off to the kitchen area.

* * * *

"Did you like Raoul fucking you that way, sweetheart?" Zeke asked.

"It was a surprise. I thought you would make me wait, which is pretty mean, if I might be permitted to say so. A girl has her needs, you know."

Zeke barked on a laugh. "Seems to me this particular girl needs to remember not to criticize her masters."

"Yes, Sir," Cantara replied, doing that cute thing of mangling her lower lip between her teeth as fire flashed through compelling eyes that had regained all their luster. "I guess she forgot."

"Get down on the rug, on your hands and knees."

While she did so, Zeke followed Raoul's example by freeing himself from the tight confines of his jeans. He still had a hard time believing they had Cantara back, thanked every deity he could name for her safe delivery, and took a moment to marvel at her powers of recovery. To have gotten her memory back, survive the attack by Romney *and* embrace their games again so quickly was nothing short of remarkable. No wonder she was their soul mate. A woman with less spirit would never have held their interest for long.

Zeke drew in a sharp breath when he glanced at the picture awaiting him on the rug. The dress rode up, exposing her bare backside, and her clamped nipples dangled invitingly beneath her. But it was the expression on Cantara's face as she sneaked a sideways glance at him from beneath her cascading hair that got to Zeke the most. Her eyes were smoky with passion, and not because Raoul had just given her a ride, but because she was anticipating what was to come next. The little tease *wanted* to be spanked, and who was Zeke to deny her?

He stepped up behind her with a birch in his hands and flexed it against his palm. It made a sharp cracking sound that easily echoed above the soft background music. He moved it gently, lovingly, across her buttocks, and then brought it down over them with moderate force, causing her to gasp, and then flinch. Raoul had abandoned the supper and was watching proceedings.

"Yeah, baby, you remember now, don't you?"

"Yes, Master."

"Are you sorry?"

"Hmm..."

Zeke brought the birch down a little harder. "How about now?"

"I think I've learned my lesson, Sir."

"Yeah, I think so, too."

Zeke kneeled behind her and lovingly kissed the places he'd just whipped, his tongue whirling, sucking, claiming ownership. He slid a couple of fingers inside her and used the other hand to slide lube down the crack in her butt. He circled her anus with a slick finger, meeting no resistance other than a sharp intake of breath when he slipped it inside.

"That's it, darlin', I'm gonna fuck your ass."

She whimpered and pushed back against his finger.

"But I got something else for you first."

He reached to one side and grabbed the studded collar he and Raoul had had made for her—studded with diamonds, that is. He reached beneath her hair and fastened it in place, then attached the chain that dangled from its D ring to the nipple clamp chain.

"There you go, honey. Just so you know, if you move your head back too fast it's gonna play havoc with those nipple clamps." Zeke chuckled. "Gotta keep you in check somehow."

Zeke added a blindfold for good measure and shared a look with Raoul, who was busy snapping pictures of Cantara on all fours, clamped up and collared, begging to have her ass fucked.

"Don't keep the lady waiting, bud," Raoul said, grinning as he ran his hand up and down his rejuvenated erection.

"Perhaps we ought to hold dinner and do this together," Zeke suggested, taking pity on his buddy.

"Good plan."

Both men stripped bare and set to work. It was Raoul who positioned himself beneath Cantara, grabbed her hips, and eased her down onto his throbbing cock. Zeke was occupied with distending her backside by increasing the number of fingers he slid into her.

"We're gonna fuck you together now," Raoul told her. "Just like you've been begging us to do. Then we're gonna have dinner, and then we're gonna spend the rest of the night fucking you some more." He sucked her lower lip into his mouth and made her gasp. "We have a problem, see. We can't seem to get enough of you, sweetheart, but then we do have three years to make up for. Are you ready for multiple orgasms?"

Cantara nodded vigorously, sending her hair dancing across his face. "Yes," she said breathlessly, not seeming to mind that the motion of her head pulled on the nipple clamps. "I want to please you both."

"Oh, you will, sugar," Zeke said from behind her in a rich, earthy voice. "Count on it."

Raoul grasped her hips a little tighter and lowered her slowly onto his cock again. Zeke knew he would impale her slowly, taking his time to savour every precious moment.

"Remember not to move and let us do all the work, darlin'," Zeke told her.

"Yes, but hurry, please. I don't think I can hold out for long."

Zeke chuckled as he slid his cock into her tight backside, working his way deeper with slow precision, closing his eyes because the pleasure was too intense to be withstood any other way. He sensed Raoul withdrawing to make room for him. Then they reversed the process like a well-oiled machine, rousing their precious baby's passions with skill and dedication to the cause. Cantara's breathing quickly fractured, as did her ability to remain passive. It seemed the orgasm Raoul had given her a few minutes previously wasn't enough to take the edge off.

"Help her out here," Zeke said to Raoul.

"I'm on it."

* * * *

Cantara was on fire with a combination of need, happiness, and spine-tingling anticipation. She felt gloriously abandoned as she submitted to her guys with joy in her heart. Everything they had suffered over the past three years had been leading up to this moment and she intended to enjoy every second of it. There would be many repeat performances over the coming years, she knew that very well, but this one would always remain in her memory. It was the one that would finally expunge all the horrors they'd lived with for so long.

She gasped as Raoul's thumb rubbed across her thrumming clit. Her sheath spasmed around his cock and she felt the familiar tingling sensation of a climax building deep within her core. She threw back her head, agitating her clamped tits in the process, and allowed it to consume her because she didn't have the strength or the will to fight against it. She came quickly and, for her, quietly, shuddering through the thrill of her desperation.

"Okay, honey," Zeke said, chuckling as he slid deeper into her backside. "Now that we have your attention…"

Raoul's cock, long and thick, slid into her pussy and then out again, making room for Zeke to pay homage to her backside. It was totally wild and Cantara simply gave herself over to the pleasure as the muscles in her belly clenched and sizzling desire built within her again at an astonishing speed.

"This what you need, sugar?"

"I sure as heck do." Cantara's limbs quivered but she somehow managed to maintain her position, even though her liquefied limbs had no muscle power left in them to support her. "Yes, you make me feel alive again, guys. Like everything we've been though has been for a reason. This reason."

"Oh, sweet darlin'," Zeke muttered.

"Okay, babe, let's take this up a notch," Raoul replied. "I can tell you got needs."

Zeke responded by plunging a little harder and deeper into her ass, his body hot and hard over hers as the fresh scent of Raoul's arousal messed with her senses. Selfish longing gripped her as they poured on the delicious torture. Every pulse point in her body came alive and a low, animalistic sound broke through the otherwise almost silent room. The sound came from her. She was keening, gasping and then begging by turn, the sharp, tangible need that gripped her too intense to be withstood passively.

"That's it, darlin'." Zeke gave her backside a sharp slap as he withdrew and Raoul took his turn to invade her cunt. "We're really fucking you now. You're getting all we have to offer you. Take what you need, honey. We're all gonna come together."

His words robbed Cantara of what little self-control she had managed to maintain. The ambience, her sexy outfit, the clamps and collar, but most of all their rock-hard cocks splitting her in two, was simply too much for her to withstand. The sensation of Zeke working her backside burned and intensified as shivers of intense excitement gripped her body and she teetered on the brink of something truly mind-blowing.

"Guys, I can't…I need—"

"Okay, darlin'," Zeke replied, his voice deep with controlled desire. "Let's do this."

Their work rate increased, Cantara's heart rate kicked up a notch and all her synapses fired in unison as her world imploded. With an uninhibited cry, she rode their cocks as her entire body went into meltdown and she felt both of them shoot their loads simultaneously, grunting and moaning for what felt like an eternity.

Spent, the three of them lay together on the floor for several minutes, their bodies bathed in thin films of perspiration as they waited for their breathing to return to a more normal rate.

"Wow!" Raoul said weakly.

"You okay, babe?" Zeke asked, leaning up on one elbow to examine her face and remove the nipple clamps.

"How can you even ask?" She managed to move just enough to kiss each of them in turn. "Thank you. I guess we needed that to slay the ghost of the past three years."

"I'll say," Raoul agreed, getting up to fetch yet another wash cloth.

She sat at the table not long after that, still wearing her tarty dress and collar. The food was delicious, but the company was way better.

"To you, darlin'," Raoul said, raising a crystal flute filled with pink vintage champagne. "And to second chances."

"To us," Cantara said, raising her glass to both of theirs. "And definitely to second chances."

"We love you, Cantara," Zeke said softly. "With all our hearts and souls. Don't ever leave us again."

"I love both of you, more than I imagined possible," she replied, brushing away fresh tears. "And you're stuck with me. I'm not planning on going anywhere."

"Good!" they replied in unison.

Both men constantly found reasons to touch her throughout the meal, feeding her small bites of food from their own forks, making a fuss of her, not allowing her to do a single thing to help herself. As soon as they had finished eating, they carried her off to bed, warning her not to expect a lot of sleep.

That was okay, she thought, as she leaned her face against the reassuringly solidity of Raoul's chest and held Zeke's hand as he walked along beside them. There would be plenty of time for the three of them to catch up on lost sleep as they grew old together.

THE END

WWW.ZARACHASE.COM

ABOUT THE AUTHOR

Zara Chase is a British author who spends a lot of her time travelling the world. Being a gypsy provides her with ample opportunities to scope out exotic locations for her stories. She likes to involve her heroines in her erotic novels in all sorts of dangerous situations—and not only with the hunky heroes whom they encounter along the way. Murder, blackmail, kidnapping and fraud make frequent appearances in her books, adding pace and excitement to her racy stories.

Zara is an animal lover who enjoys keeping fit and is on a one-woman mission to keep the wine industry ahead of the recession.

For all titles by Zara Chase, please visit
www.bookstrand.com/zara-chase

Siren Publishing, Inc.
www.SirenPublishing.com

Lightning Source UK Ltd.
Milton Keynes UK
UKOW06f2154050615

252993UK00015B/277/P